digital
DARLING
AN AMERICAN STORY

Rick Roberts

BABY BOOMER
P R E S S

BABY BOOMER
P R E S S

Published by Baby Boomer Press LLC.

Visit BabyBoomerPress.com, or write:
Baby Boomer Press LLC, PO Box 1987, Windham, ME 04062

Printed in the United States of America
Design: Neville Design, Braintree, MA

First paperback and e-book editions
June 2011
10 9 8 7 6 5 4

ISBN: trade paperback: 978-0-9749659-1-8
Library of Congress Control Number: 2011908391

Acknowledgements

Many friends, relatives and associates have contributed to this work. First among them, my parents who encouraged me to think freely and provided the luxury of time to do so. Thanks to my writing group in Maine who generously kept this story on track for years. To my eagle-eyed editors, Katherine Paul, Lindsay Tice and Janet Neville. To Kurt Vonnegut Jr. whose wonderful work and insightful words ("I tell you we are here on Earth to fart around, and don't let anybody tell you different.") are sustaining. Finally, thanks to America which gave me the freedom to roam and plenty to look at.

digital
DARLING
AN AMERICAN STORY

Part One

"There are too many pigs for the tits."

– Abraham Lincoln

First interrogation
Breakfast appetizers

For a week they gave Seamus enough water and sleep to still get a straight answer out of him. At dawn on the seventh morning two large men ushered him from his cell into an interrogation room and sat him down at one end of a worn linoleum table. At the other end, a sandy-haired man with his glasses pushed up over a large forehead flipped through the contents of a manila folder, apparently refreshing himself with its contents.

It wasn't the first time Seamus had sat at this end of the table. He knew it wasn't the most inhospitable accommodations the National Security Agency could provide. He took the initiative in defining the terms of his own defense.

"She wasn't real," he said. "Just an image."

The NSA interrogator looked up and gave Seamus a wry smile. "She was dangerous."

"Digital Darling didn't have political aspirations."

"She built a constituency."

They argued the point all day. Seamus changed tactics. "How serious is the agency?"

The man flipped down his glasses. "Treason. Right here

in writing."

Seamus sighed through a smile. "All this for a digital cocktail. She's gone—out of the public eye."

The interrogator didn't bite. "Virtual reality can program the brain as permanently as real experience," he said. "Wouldn't bet my appeal against it."

"How long are we going to do this?" Seamus asked.

"There are six of us. We're on shifts."

Seamus made a clicking sound with his tongue. "What do you want to hear?"

"Your side. No promises—some important people are dead."

Seamus sat up straight.

"I'd like some bacon and eggs."

The sandy-haired man nodded at the mirrored wall and flipped his hand palm up as if to say, do it.

Seamus poured himself a glass of water from the plastic pitcher on the table and rubbed the stubble on his chin. "It all started with her father, Bartholomew Brand," he began. "You know who he was, right?"

Chapter 1
Personal mobility
solutions

The fifteen swimsuit models onboard shuddered and cried out as the Boeing 370 business jet dipped sharply to the left. The weary pilot brought the plane around to runway 2N-1 at Lindbergh International Field in San Diego. He pulled back on the throttle.

"Got her now, Cap," his exhausted co-pilot encouraged him.

They had been airborne for thirteen agonizing hours non-stop from Borneo, everyone onboard desperately ill—one, a hairstylist who had joined the calendar shoot in Los Angeles, already dead in his seat.

The chartered jet taxied to a stop at 6:03 AM on another promising spring day in southern California. The hysterical passengers rushed down the plane's stairway and into the moist dawn air. Two collapsed on the tarmac. As the others, some coughing up blood, approached the terminal an alert security guard blocked their path.

Chapter 2
Politics is flat

President Alexander North, former chancellor of the University of Arizona, heir to a cattle fortune and author of two best sellers on American history, was swept into office by a broad constituency of disillusioned Americans willing at last to abandon the traditional two-party system. North ran and was elected as an Independent. Tall, handsome and unusually gregarious for an academic, he made a nostalgic three-word promise the signature of his campaign—*Democracy's Best Chance*. Two years later on a crackerjack January day, he stood on the White House's southern steps, right hand high in the air and became only the second candidate ever elected to the nation's highest office without the support of a major political party. The other was George Washington.

North was four months into the job.

The morning of the San Diego incident, his schedule was interrupted and he was called to the Situation Room beneath the West Wing. He entered the main conference area where his Emergency Response Team had already assembled.

"What's our status?" he asked.

"Twenty-one confirmed dead, Mr. President," the secretary of transportation spoke up first. "All but two of the models, the captain, co-pilot and three other passengers on the charter. One was DOA. We've lost nine more at the airport, including two security guards, the airport manager and three businessmen unlucky enough to have chartered the same jet on its next leg." The secretary looked down and shook her head. "They boarded before anyone knew what the Sam Hill was going on. The agency's apologies, sir."

The national security advisor, head of the response team, piped up when North met his eyes. "Some of the charter passengers were coughing up blood when they disembarked," he said. "They were stopped from entering the terminal."

"If they were kept outside how did it spread so fast?" the president asked.

"The same guard who stopped them caught it. He eventually went inside. He's among the dead, so details are a little sketchy. We'll make sure he gets recognized, sir."

"Not for spreading the bug," the president said grimly. "How long were the passengers sick?"

"Up to 13 hours, sir," said the transportation secretary. "Flight time for a Boeing 370 Business Jet across the Pacific."

"And now we're losing them in, what—less than an hour?" North asked. "What are we dealing with?"

"Prelim from Atlanta is Class 5 virus," the team CDC representative spoke up. "Airborne. Contagious as hell. Remarkably fast. It may have evolved once already. That may explain the quick deaths at the airport."

"Any good news?"

"We threw a net over the plane and the contaminated terminal, of course. Our response team is on location. We'll have labs by end of day. We're testing those who didn't die on the trip too, hoping to find out why. There's this: Any bug that moves this fast tends to burn out fast."

"If it's contained," the president said, thinking an international airport was an incubator. Then, after a moment scanning the report before him, North looked back up. "Sports Illustrated?"

"Yes, Mr. President. The annual calendar shoot. Routine Time Inc. charter. All Americans," said Communications Director Pipes Barronson.

"Where are we, right this minute?" North asked.

The transportation secretary continued. "We quarantined everyone we could stop. That number is high. Several thousand. Word got out, of course."

North squinted.

"Cell phones," the secretary said. "The local police have stopped all traffic around Lindbergh. No one is getting in or out now. There's been a lot of, well, panic. Things will be bad out there for a while."

"Worse case?" North asked.

The CDC rep answered. "An outbreak in an urban area could rack up some scary numbers. Hospitals would be overwhelmed. Fear would lead to violence sooner than anyone likes to admit."

"We've got two battalions of the California National Guard waiting for your order, sir," the national security advisor said.

"Military weapons aimed at frightened citizens?" North asked disapprovingly. "Sounds like Kent State. Or the '68 Democratic Convention. Sounds like what we bitch at everyone else for doing."

The transportation secretary took a private phone call then looked around the room obviously concerned. "We've got outbreaks at O'Hare and Logan."

The president turned to his communications director. "Get me some air time, Pipes."

Chapter 3
Networked life

B ack in 1850, Bartholomew's great grandfather, Ernest Brand, bought 120 acres of shorefront on Big Sebago Lake in Maine over the protest of the local Passamaquoddy Indians who claimed the land by prior use. He erected what he called a "Tudor cabin," sighting it to afford a panoramic view of the lake's broadest expanse. Not reaching too deep, he named the property *Wide Waters*. Barns, outbuildings and a guest-house followed in due course. As did a commercial-sized dock, the end of which was an ideal spot to monitor the steady flotilla of logs on their way to the paper mills of Westbrook downstream. A fact not lost on Ernest who built the family fortune on lumber losing only half of it at the poker table where one night on the third raise he died of consumption.

The property had been occupied by successive generations of the Brand family right up to Bartholomew, his late wife and his daughter, Carmen. The original Tudor cabin had evolved into a manor house rich in architectural details—cut glass windows, a slate roof, a fine summer porch across the front, and a half dozen stately white pillars to hold it all up. The local historical registered had nicknamed the home The White House on the Lake. To maintain it, Bartholomew employed nearly three-dozen Passamaquoddy as stable hands, craftsmen and gardeners, maintenance and security men.

Bartholomew now poured himself an early evening bourbon then sank so deeply into his favorite club chair he could almost count the change under the cushion. He channel surfed the monitor on his desk across the room. He checked the financial headlines; stopped by the Golf Channel, as it was Master's Week. News of the SI calendar flight was on every other channel.

"A chartered plane inbound from Borneo," one news anchor said, "touched down at Lindbergh International Field early yesterday morning. According to eyewitnesses, the arriving passengers—ten members of a film crew and fifteen swimsuit models were desperately ill. Several, we've been informed, have since died. Sources inside the airport say there have been additional casualties on the ground, including airport personnel. Whatever disease those folks were carrying back from Southeast Asia, it was deadly. Very deadly."

Behind the on-scene reporter, video captured the siren-fueled crisis still unfolding in San Diego.

"Has the airport been shut down?" the studio anchor asked his reporter.

"Yes," he said. "Incoming flights have been diverted. All outbound flights have been cancelled. Lindbergh is swarming with police and swat teams. Some are wearing germ warfare suits. We're told that the mood inside the airport has turned ugly. Frankly, it's going to take more than the TSA to contain the thousands being held inside Terminal B against their will."

Bartholomew drained his glass.

"The onrushing pandemic has arrived," he scoffed.

He reached behind him and pressed a button hidden on the back of the club chair. A section of bookcases across the room slid aside revealing a large well-lit room.

The former head of the New Media Lab at the Massachusetts Institute of Technology lifted himself up and walked through the opening in the wall. "Let's see what web bot has to say about this," he said.

Chapter 4
Anticipatory self-defense

The normally busy White House briefing room was empty except for two invited cameramen and a few executive staffers. North didn't want to field questions so the White House Press Corps hadn't been invited. The president stood at the podium in the front of the room and tested his mic. A sharp looking brunette in an Armani jumpsuit dabbed his forehead with a powder puff.

At 8 PM, the presidential seal dissolved into North's image and he delivered the speech that would define his administration:

"Fellow citizens," he said, "many of you already know about the tragic events that transpired in San Diego yesterday. A privately chartered jet, inbound from the Far East, landed at Lindbergh Field early Tuesday morning. The crew and most of the 25 people on board—all Americans—were exhibiting severe flu-like symptoms when they touched down. Tonight, I regret to inform you that most of those passengers and many others at Lindbergh Field have died. Our Center for

Disease Control is on the scene. They have labeled this scourge an unknown Class 5 virus—easily transmitted through the air, highly contagious. A killer. I'm speaking to you tonight because earlier today I learned there have been additional outbreaks at our airports in Chicago and Boston. And I'm afraid, more casualties."

The president paused to let the words sink in. "There is no vaccine, and no way to forecast how long it will take to develop one. Our strategy is containment. Accordingly, I am asking every American to stay home. Cancel your travel plans. If you are on the road, please return home immediately. Effective tomorrow at midnight, all non-emergency airline traffic will stop. Incoming international flights are being rerouted as I speak. Let me repeat that: in just over twenty-four hours, all non-essential air travel within the United States will be grounded. Exemptions will be considered on a case-by-case basis and handled on-line by a federal task force."

A collective gasp came from the few people in the room. The president paused again, then continued. "This office is fully aware of the consequences of such a drastic step. And taking it without more advanced notice," he said. "Government at all levels will work closely with leaders of those industries most directly impacted by the shutdown. The CDC has advised that a viral strain this fast acting may also prove to be short-lived. It may burn itself out quickly. There is no cause for general panic. We have faced similar outbreaks successfully in the past. Continue to go to work and travel within your community. We are doing everything possible to keep this disruption to our physical and economic health as brief as possible. All traditional news outlets and appropriate Internet sites will receive updates on our progress. Naturally, this travel restriction will be lifted at the first opportunity."

North leaned forward, almost imperceptively. He stared into the lights and spoke in measured terms.

"Tonight I'm asking every American to accept their civic responsibility. To cooperate with each other and find alternatives to long-distance travel. Further, to use your influence and position to persuade those around you to do the same. What we need now is nation-wide collective action. The well-being of the country depends upon it. I'm asking each of you to put aside any personal inconvenience caused by this temporary ban. Look deep inside where you keep your love for our great land and ask: What does it mean to be a patriot? What does it mean right this minute? Then make the right decision. Good night, fellow Americans. God bless, and thank you."

Chapter 5
End times

"I can tell the mood of the blacksmith from the strike of his hammer," Seamus wrote home one Christmas from Sturbridge Village. His mother never answered. Instead, he received a registered envelope from the state of Pennsylvania explaining that his parents had died in a small plane crash off the coast of Cancun. The accident was attributed to black-market engine parts. An investigation had been unproductive; the family's small estate was in probate. There would be no funeral. Regrettably the bodies were lost to sharks.

A year passed, Seamus' tenth as resident potter at the Massachusetts tourist attraction, when he received a second registered letter. This one from a Philadelphia lawyer he didn't know containing a cashier's check for $10,000. He was the sole heir. Unable to spend the money, he carried it around for months in the fifth pocket in his jeans. Finally, he bought the only thing he ever really wanted—a horse, a handsome broad-shouldered gray mare with a white face and stockings.

He was sure the animal was made of porcelain. He

named her Dobson after the English poet. Every day they rode into his 18th Century world, the gentle breeze flapping across his overalls, combing through the soft needle fabric of the forest. In sunshine, rain, knee-deep in snow, horse and rider made the daily pilgrimage from his rented room to his potter's shed, and back again. Between trips, the mare enjoyed hay barns, lush pastures and the company of other horses. Every morning, the thump of Dobson's hooves anchored Seamus to the place.

The day was turning cool with sundown and Seamus was thinking about hot cider when a handful of tourists filed into his shed. They wandered about examining his wares—shelf upon shelf of tankards and goblets and carafes, his crocks and planters and pails. He was famous for his vases. They were earthenware, or leather hard, or bone dry. They were crafted from the perfect red clay he dug from the bottom of the Housatonic River. His throaty charm and sentimental tales about life in the Village contributed to their popularity. Many had found their way into private collections.

Drying his hands on his apron, Seamus offered a welcoming smile as the tourists bunched up before him. He launched into his spiel.

"In the Village, the potter soon needs the blacksmith's art...and the fletcher's, the weaver's, the cooper's." He spoke softly so they would listen harder. His hesitant phrasing and the rhythm of his wheel lulled the visitors back in time.

Seamus seldom looked up as they had paid to watch him. Rather, he made a fuss of rearranging his drying slabs and wooden braces. He reached down and with a sigh lifted up an oaken bucket filled with well water, cupped one hand and splashed some on the back of his neck. He worked in an open, handmade cotton shirt and perspired freely before the glazing stone and hot kiln.

Two girls in the group giggled as if sharing a teenage secret.

"Where are you from?" one asked boldly.

"From the soil," Seamus said, kneading the moist clay, pressing it down in the center, lifting it slowly from the outside.

"What will you put in the pot?" the other wanted to know.

Seamus pumped the wheel. The clay spun faster. He answered, "I will put this thought. When you are young and strong, handle the good earth with care. Then, when you are old and tired and return to sleep inside her, she'll be as familiar as your childhood bed."

The girls giggled, but rewarded Seamus with admiring smiles.

The tourists whispered among themselves.

The clay whirled on.

Seamus sliced off the top inch of the new pot with a wire and cleverly shaped a handle. The onlookers were amused and he worked hard to convince them that this recreation of old New England was as much religion as folklore, a miracle not just a spectacle.

"You do not talk about the pot until it is finished," he told the visitors, "or it will crack."

Wisdom from the Hopi Indians. And his exit line. As

usual, it satisfied the crowd, many of whom had cheerfully paid the Village's steep admission price in hopes of unearthing some ancient truth, discovering some long-forgotten notion resident in this authentic replica as surely as it must have attended the original time and place. They filed out back into the time-frozen enchantment the Village was famous for.

Seamus got up behind them and watched from the shed doorway. He searched the nearby fields for Dobson's silhouette but it had grown too dark. Surrounded by his art and this unchanging world, protected by time itself, he was sure of the earth he stood on. He fantasized about living at Sturbridge forever, becoming a crotchety old man with bad knees and failing eyesight, sitting on benches and logs, dispensing wooden-bucket wisdom, letting his talented hands do some of the talking. He was 55 and would be buried in the fields Dobson loved. He had already picked out the spot.

He was blind-sided by news the Village might be in trouble.

Billy, son of the couple who operated the gristmill, ran by and called out that the president had just made a special announcement on TV. He was stopping people from traveling. Everyone had to stay home.

Stop people from moving around the country? Put tourist attractions like Sturbridge out of business at the beginning of the summer season? Surely young Billy had it wrong, Seamus told himself. The Village was hugely profitable and his pottery shed was one of its most lucrative attractions. Surely they were safe from the social fabric unraveling outside the Village's rambling stonewalls.

"Nonsense!" Seamus called after the lad. Ban travel? Preposterous. Sturbridge closed? It couldn't be true for the most compelling of reasons: he simply had no place to go.

Chapter 6
This is Ted Koppel.
Inside the casket.

As usual Carmen woke at dawn. A stiff northwest breeze cooled by the vast waters of Big Sebago Lake rustled the curtains around her open bedroom window. She could hear her horse Peppermint whinnying out in the barn. He was anxious to begin their morning ride. She dressed, washed her face at the bedroom vanity, and downstairs in the kitchen filled a cup from the fresh pot of coffee. She stepped out onto the home's big front porch and paused to watch the early sun wash over the lake.

The barn was located at the far end of a large oval driveway that linked the estate's main buildings. Joseph, her father's headman was also up early and handed Carmen the reins to Peppermint when she came in. The stocky black thoroughbred nuzzled her in greeting. She grabbed the reins as Joseph hoisted her up into the saddle. She put the horse right into a trot. Together they quickly cleared the turnout and corals and moved up across the open meadows that terraced above the lake. Horse and rider were gone in a blink, swirling pollen in their wake.

Carmen thought she'd be early for the reading of her Uncle Brad's will, but by the time she got back from riding and brushed down Peppermint several of the family's inner circle had already gathered in the formal dining room at Wide Waters. Most had been in town before North's ban went into effect. She smiled politely at Aunt Lottie, the grieving widow, and among only a handful of surviving members of the Brand family. Carmen found a seat in the unoccupied front row of chairs.

Gazing up at the arts and crafts chandeliers and the folk art decorating the walls, Carmen realized she hadn't been in the room for weeks. Ever since the unexpected death of her mother from cancer many years ago, she and her father had dined in the cozier media room. They rarely entertained. After years of house arrest, Bartholomew was prone to irritability, sometimes genuine rage, and Carmen wasn't about to make this public. For years since she had remained at his side like a trusted six-shooter, protecting his flank, intervening with authorities, occasionally taking a shot across the bow of a curious interloper. She was unmarried, childless and 44. Today was her birthday. She hoped her father had remembered. She hoped Uncle Brad had, too.

A handful of friends and family business associates filed in, each appropriately pious and no doubt praying for their share of Brad's considerable fortune. Bartholomew arrived last. His approaching footsteps echoed off the granite floors and hid in the hallway armor. All chitchat ceased as he entered the dining hall.

Carmen turned and watched her father with pride. Salt-and-pepper handsome, amicably paunched, he still carried himself with the élan that had character-ized his reign as king of the digerati, the public face of the Massachusetts Institute of Technology. He marched down the center of the room and took a seat next to her. He nodded to the family lawyer who stood fidgeting behind the music stand that served as a podium at the front of the room.

The stout solicitor patted his forehead with a hand-kerchief and gathered himself. "In the matter of the Bradford Perry estate," he began, "To my beloved wife, Lottie, I leave title to our home in Damariscotta and all accounts in our name placed in financial institutions headquartered in Maine. To my partner, Buddy, I leave my interests in the shipyard Perry & Stoneman and best wishes for Godspeed. To my niece, Carmen, I leave the property located at 346 Beacon Street in Boston, and all funds in the Perry name held by the State Street Bank & Trust Company, also in Boston."

Before the lawyer could reach again for his handker-chief, Aunt Lottie let out an angry yelp that pierced the scattered murmuring. Shaking, she pointed an accusing finger at Carmen, stammered something unintelligible but clearly profane, and then collapsed. Eventually she left the room supported by her driver and her gaggle of friends from Damariscotta.

Carmen stared at her aunt but said nothing. She knew her aunt had long suspected there was something going on between her and her husband and probably took his final testimony as proof. She realized she was squeezing her father's hand with all her might. She glanced up at him, eyes wide with exasperation as she released her grip.

⟹⟸

Bartholomew knew the real reason for his brother-in-law's generosity: Carmen had saved her uncle's business. It was not Bradford but Carmen who successfully moved the enterprise from wood and fiberglass to aluminum and steel, from privately purchased fishing boats to government-sponsored cruise ships, ferries and a raft of research vessels, one commissioned to find out where all the fish had gone. It was Carmen who seduced an international cadre of millionaires to consider her uncle's arguably modest shipbuilding business for their custom yachts. Schmoozing them in their native tongues, often recalling her visits to their hometowns and enchanted ports. She buttered up their pride and promised to bring their imaginations to life with Stoneman & Perry craftsmanship.

Bartholomew looked at his daughter in dismay. He was privy to his brother-in-law's finances—namely, that the monies held in Maine would keep Lottie stuffed with salmon and comfortably wrapped in Irish lace, but the real family wealth, the enormous sums accumulated by generations of Boston-based Perrys, was held in Boston. Still an innocent in his eyes, his daughter was suddenly, wildly rich. He had feared this day would come. Money meant freedom. That much money meant losing her.

Chapter 7
A tea party

The next day was warm and spring-like in the nation's capital. The cherry blossoms had popped and it seemed everyone was in a good mood.

President North could hear glasses clinking through the open window in the Oval Office. He got up from his desk and looked out toward the Rose Garden where the First Lady was entertaining.

"Who are they?" he asked.

Bud Wilkins, his chief of staff and former fraternity brother at Northern Arizona, looked over his shoulder. "Non-profits," he said. "Heart disease, Alzheimer's, the cancer crowd."

"Looks like they've been having tea with first ladies for a long time," North said.

"Ain't no money in the cure," Wilkins replied, quoting comedian Chris Rock.

Exactly right, North thought to himself. Careful fixing anything. There ain't no money in the cure.

The thought was interrupted by the confident triple knock of his private secretary. She peeked around the door. "Your economic affairs council is here, Mr. President."

"How do they look?

"Glum," she said.

"Send'em in anyway," North replied. "Bud, stick around for this."

The visitors, the government's best economic theorists, arranged themselves on the facing couches in the president's office. The head of the Federal Reserve came right to the point: G-20 was orchestrating a run on the dollar. The consequences would be catastrophic.

"They've taken a united stand on how we've handled the debt crisis," the Fed chairman said.

"That is to say, not handled it," said North.

"Exactly, Mr. President. Making dollars cheaper has kept our exports strong at the expense of their recoveries."

"Are we sure about this?" North asked.

"CIA sourced this," said the treasury secretary. "Scanning for keyword coincidence."

"How many votes have we got?" North said growing perturbed.

"As few as six," said the Fed chairman. "You'll recall, Mr. President, G-20 has no international authorization, no constitution. They're just the heads of state, like yourself, and ministers of finance and the like who've agreed to act together to manage the world's economy. Simply put, they've decided it's time to end the dominance of the dollar. With that in mind, we're not counting France, South Korea, or even Saudi Arabia."

North had become aware of how fragile the American Dream had become during the election. How it all might come tumbling down. An unforeseen accident like losing your health insurance. An upside-down mortgage and a pink slip. This wasn't a few blocks of three-beds, three-baths outside Las Vegas. This was middle class families of four living in motel rooms across the country. Where was he going to get enough hope?

"When?" was all he could ask.

"We can't give you the exact date," the chairman said. "We don't think they have one."

"What will it look like?"

"It will be over in a day," the secretary of treasury said. "Let's say they decide to put twenty-five percent of our currency back into circulation. The markets open Asia. Central banks start dumping. Billions. Eventually trillions. The value of the dollar could drop forty even fifty percent. We won't be in a position to stop it. The later markets have to sell lower than those who sold at first so everyone agrees upfront on a restitution formula. That's the detail that tipped the plot."

North asked again, "When?"

"Best guess is by year-end," said the Fed chairman. "Earlier if we don't stop printing money."

The six members of the council sat like carnival dummies hoping no one hit them with a baseball, or dart.

"An attack on our currency is an act of war," the treasury secretary said mildly.

"We don't have enough enemies?" North asked rhetorically. "Now we bomb our trading partners?"

The president got up and paced around the room. Healthcare, welfare, retirement benefits and pension plans were all backed by phantom budgets. So were disaster relief efforts, infrastructure and environmental expenses, educational initiatives, even veteran's benefits. Government financing was beyond dysfunctional. Insane, really. It operated on over-optimistic projections, outdated economic formulas, unfounded confidence in Washington's ability to control business cycles. It routinely doubled favorable numbers and cut contrary ones in half. Anything that didn't add up was simply carried off the books. The country now borrowed one of every two dollars it spent. That debt financing had been sleeping with fiscal irresponsibility for decades was the worst kept secret in Washington. Only the general public remained largely uninformed and complacent.

"How much do we owe?" North asked.

The head of the GAO put a number on it. "We're bright red from top to bottom, Mr. President. If you include all non-funded obligations, so-called deferred revenues, the nation's obligations total well over 130 trillion dollars over the life of our bonds."

"We advertise a tenth of that."

"Yes sir, more or less..."

"And the world no longer believes us," North intoned. "Imagine that!"

"We have some suggestions to buy time," the Fed chairman said.

North stepped toward the middle of the gathering and kicked the bottom of the antique Jeffersonian tea table. Cups and saucers flew everywhere.

"Isn't buying time what got us into this goddamn fix?" he yelled. "Bubbles blowing bubbles. Somebody say it!"

No one would.

Finally the treasury secretary whispered, "Default."

Plague and now bankruptcy. Bankruptcy and plague. People were dying horrible deaths and now the cost of everything from milk to blue jeans was about to double overnight. The twin nightmares rolled around inside North's head like gutter balls. They would overwhelm his legacy.

It was bitter news for a man who imagined his strong jaw carved out of the stone at Mt. Rushmore.

Chapter 8
Ideas don't keep

North couldn't sleep. He struggled with his bad luck. A deadly virus and now, drowning in debt. Why did they co-exist? Did they have something in common? Could he jam them together somehow?

He slipped out of the bed where his wife, Eliza, slept peacefully and wandered down the main hallway in the upstairs residence. He talked to himself out loud, dismissing one strategy after another. He nodded at the Secret Service guard at one end of the hall, did an about face and started back down the corridor. About halfway he sat down heavily in the Windsor chair under the portrait of Abe Lincoln outside his famous bedroom. Like Lincoln, North was determined to keep a feeling of helplessness from creeping into the public consciousness. Like Lincoln, he understood that a nation both heart sick and broke was a sitting duck. He drifted into a restless sleep. He dreamed about American children clad in gas masks, taking bus tours through ganglands and wastelands hosted by militia groups turned tour guides. Everyone was armed and singing "Ain't no money in the cure."

Just after daybreak, his chief of staff gently tapped on his shoulder. "Good morning, Mr. President," Wilkins said.

North opened his eyes to a pale pink dawn streaming through the sheer curtains.

"Morning, Bud. What's up?"

The president's best friend gave him a sympathetic smile. "Alex, I'm afraid we've had some bad news."

———————

When North found out that the virus had moved out of airport corridors into suburban neighborhoods, he went back on TV that night. He extended the ban on air travel indefinitely and called up the National Guard to close down the nation's Interstate system by the end of the week.

Again, he didn't take questions from the press.

Chapter 9
The smartest guy
in the room

"Relentless bastards," Bartholomew fumed. He rapped his knuckles on his office desk. *Go home and shut up* was what North really meant. Bartholomew had made the president's acquaintance years earlier. They had been on opposing sides of an academic debate. North held that governments must reserve the right to manage the private lives of its citizens as population densities grew and technologies allowed. Bartholomew countered that history was filled with soul-crushing despots making similar arguments. Elaborate prison systems were their primary legacy.

Web bot was betting against North, too. Pandemics ran in 30-year cycles and this wasn't one of them. What was the president up to? What big lie was it this time? They already knew where you were, what you were doing, and whom you were doing it with. The day after 9/11, the US federal government embarked on a massive data-collection program. The idea was to gather information at the street level and push it up through a series of human and artificial intelligence filters attempting to identify anything threatening before it became operational.

It was all about street smarts.

Traffic violations, the recordings from public cameras, scans of license plates taken in shopping center parking lots, the location and content of cell phone conversations, Internet activity, personal habits and health records, financial data, every diet you'd been on and the name of every dog you'd ever owned was being aggregated and examined at dozens of so-called fusion centers. Innumerable intelligence agencies had front row seats to the daily lives of private citizens just for the asking. Ordinary people were being assigned risk ratings. It was all quietly financed by the federal government and buried in a variety of offices with forgettable acronyms for names. And no one was objecting.

Bartholomew got up and pressed the button behind the club chair.

"I'll show you what it means to be a patriot," he said, closing the wall of books behind him.

He paced around in the lab, thumbing through notebooks, muttering invectives.

He had routinely used the lab at Wide Waters as a backup site for his work at MIT, so he left the university with most of his research intact. And it was safe. The laboratory at the lake was hidden within the architectural irregularities of the expanded manor house. Over the centuries the room had sequestered runaway slaves, munitions, whiskey, cash, and whiskey again when in 1871 the state passed the Maine Law which banned drinks sold by the shot. Under Bartholomew's guiding hand the large secret room had been transformed into a communications complex: world-wired, self-contained and steel encased. A battle-ready bunker. Even the small assemblage of antennae and exhaust vents on the roof had been camouflaged.

What counter-move was possible?

Bartholomew's attention turned to the shelves holding a collection of videotapes that the Brand family photographer, Casaba Rendor, had taken during his infamous lecture tours. Mostly the tapes captured the carefree life of his daughter and traveling companion, a winsome teenaged Carmen.

"Sit closer," Bartholomew would say, as they rested on ancient foundations, famous ruins, historic ramparts.

"She's probably learning more with you, anyway," said the understanding headmasters of private schools, as Carmen dazzled them with her command of foreign phrases, as Bartholomew explained the importance of his lectures, reason enough for her extended absences.

"The camera is your friend," Casaba assured her with every frame. In his adoring Hungarian immigrant eye she was bee honey blonde from tip to toe, slender, graceful, and compliant. He captured her vulnerability and her surprising boldness. Her eyes were curious and hazel, her sharp bones visible, her mouth small but lips full. He filmed her splashing in the surf on Omaha Beach, playing with lion cubs on the plains of Kalahari, petting the six-toed cats on the front porch of Hemmingway's house in Key West. She met cowboys and commodores with equal ease. She danced under the stars on five continents. She caught the eye of both young and grown men, and when she was 16, *Luna Cornea*, Mexico's famous photo magazine, ran her picture on its cover. Semi-clad in diaphanous white linen, Carmen's hands were joined in namaste as she bowed before a backdrop of Mayan pyramids at sunrise. The issue was widely distributed at an archeology conference hosted by Harvard University and that summer the cover found its way onto the walls of yachts and fishing boats from New Bedford to Halifax.

Heady days. Carmen, the darling of international salons; Bartholomew, the go-to guy on the alternate digital world taking shape on Internetworks.

He was still stunned at how fast it all turned upside down. Once the mouthpiece of MIT, his lectures suddenly seen as subversive not instructive. Their firebrand author dangerous not just famous. Riots, authorities insisted, the direct result of his persuasiveness about the potential misuse of data. MIT was encouraged by Washington to solve the problem. As an institution heavily endowed with public money, the university didn't anguish over its decision to do its part for national security. That was 25 years ago. Every day since, the words "Go home and shut up," burned in Bartholomew ears.

He sat down at the lab's main console. With the push of a few buttons he brought three Macintosh portables online. He used Macs because the government used PCs. That bought time.

On the first Mac he began a broad search for every recorded mention of his daughter anywhere, at any time. On the second, he used a media transfer program to digitize Casaba's film and systematically load it onto an outboard memory.

Then he logged onto the dark web and pirated an unguarded router somewhere in N. Korea. Once owned, he ported the router to the second Mac and programmed an uplink that allowed only transmissions that mimicked a dynamically generated database—that is, one that evolved by moving and could travel without any hyper-text attached. To would-be eavesdroppers, such traffic was not a defined signal, but rather a low hum, a bland digital tone that was everywhere the same, and nowhere in particular. The messages used the Internet's source code as a channel. It was source code Bartholomew had authored and buried so deep it would take years to find and decode it. There would be no way to trace the source of a broadcast from the second Mac. Then he dedicated the rest of the second computer as a broadcast studio, complete with acoustical mixing and blazing graphics. Into the last Mac, he dumped the software he'd been writing in his banishment. The most advanced life repli-cation software in the world. Software that might, in the right hands, upset the balance of power in America.

He was half done.

Back on the first Mac, a digital sequencer or hack-er's dictionary had been plowing through the endless number-letter combinations that guarded access to the world's databases. It was patiently finding and eras-ing every pixel that referenced Carmen Brand of Wide Waters, Maine. It destroyed her birth certificate, school reports, driving record, social security number, every reference to every book ever borrowed from the library. Press coverage, her modeling career, credit and bank references and electronic purchases all disappeared. As did her extensive network of social media links and messages. Through an exhaustive keyword search, the software cross-referenced the Brand and Perry family histories, destroying any mention of Carmen's name or image, any hint of her role in the family business, or place on the family tree. Retracing every step, it eradicated any reference to her during Bartholomew's expansive career at MIT. Then it did the same thing for the home she inherited in Boston. When the scorching ceased, Carmen had never sent a single email, never touched the keyboard of a computer or dialed a smart phone. She was dead to the digital world, and the brownstone at 346 Beacon belonged to no one.

Bartholomew had played his last ace.

It was dawn.

He sat back and second-guessed his work. Had he created the platform for a new form of multi-dimensional entertainment that might capture the attention of the world? Or something so powerful it would make his daughter a target? He didn't underestimate what a starving bureaucracy was capable of in the name of self-preservation. He balanced this thought with his festering hate for the centralized authority that had crushed his career.

⟩⟩●⟨⟨

Back from her morning ride, Carmen was surprised to find her father awake in his office. "Up late, or up early?" she asked.

"Both."

"I'll be back with coffee."

She returned with two cups and took a seat on one corner of the big Victorian library table that served as his desk.

He smiled and Carmen noticed his eyes were red. Had he been crying?

"What is it, father?"

"Real progress is never made by large organizations," Bartholomew said. "Social justice can only be safeguarded by bold individual action."

It wasn't the first time she'd heard this.

"We go about our daily routines," her father went on, "minimizing surprise. Keeping our balance. The human psyche is fragile, easily upset. Events tumble down around us and sometimes we break. Sometimes the whole damn world breaks around us."

"Daddy, what have you been up to?"

"I want you to go to Boston."

Carmen couldn't believe her ears. The thought had been on her mind since she'd inherited the brownstone. She had wanted to suggest it, but was reluctant to leave him alone. Did they suddenly agree about this?

"Why now?"

"Your country is under attack."

Carmen searched his eyes. Had the old spark returned? Over the years, she had witnessed flashes of determination. Some were driven by the madness of his confinement; others reflected the clear light of genius. Even if the travel ban was no longer temporary, wasn't it still a reasonable response? The kill rate of the virus was almost fifty percent. What did he know, or what did he suspect?

"There's no virus?" she asked her father.

"Oh, there's a virus. But the attack comes from within."

"So the ban is a ruse?"

"Remember when Thoreau was in jail," Bartholomew said, "and his friend asked him what he was doing in there?"

"Yes. And Thoreau asked his friend what he was doing out there," Carmen said with a laugh. With her father it was always about resistance.

Then Carmen noticed for the first time the three Mac laptops stacked up on the desk and a large white envelope with her name on it. "You've devised some clever way for us to stay in touch?"

Bartholomew lifted himself up and came around to where she sat. "There's some paperwork from State Street Bank. Deal only with James Holliston."

"Hardly a good time to travel," Carmen said, testing him one last time.

Bartholomew let out a grunt.

"OK, summer in the city," she said finally. "There's no telling what mischief you've gotten me into, but I'll go."

Bartholomew hugged his daughter for a long time. Tears rolled down his cheeks. He knew it wasn't going to be that easy.

"Happy birthday," he said, giving his daughter the gift of freedom.

———————≫●≪———————

Before leaving the lab, Bartholomew sent an encrypted file to his former lab partner at MIT, Day-to-day Dave: *Carmen coming to Boston immediately. Concept attached. Pick up where we left off. At last, BB.*

Chapter 10
Lipitor® isn't for everyone

The next day Seamus and eighty-five other residents of the ongoing period play known as Sturbridge Village sat together in stunned silence. They had assembled at the request of the attraction's director in the wake of the President North's startling announcement. The director explained that Sturbridge, like any top-line attraction, was dependent on visitors arriving by plane and out of state. They could not operate profitably during a travel ban, so the time would be used to make capital investment and repairs rather than host a mere handful of tourists.

Besides, it was our patriotic duty, the director reminded everyone.

"Bridge paychecks would be issued in the morning," the man said. "Events such as unscheduled shutdowns were clearly covered in your contracts..."

Blah, blah.

The director encouraged everyone to contact their Congressional representatives urging a return to normalcy. The Village would re-open at the earliest possible date. When, exactly, wasn't clear.

Seamus nudged the village seamstress who was sitting next to him.

"I'm going to Disney World," she said.

Seamus understood she would be accepting a long-standing offer to join Disney's Imagineering Department as costume maker. Rumor was Disney might buck the ban. Seamus couldn't imagine Dobson, or himself, living in the muck of Florida.

Back outside they shared hugs and happy trails with their friends and neighbors.

⸺⸺⸺◦⸺⸺⸺

Seamus left Dobson with the herd and walked home alone to the small room and bath he rented in the back of a hotel outside the Village's main entrance. He opened the front door that he never locked and sat down heavily on the bed. Next to him was part of Dobson's harness he was reworking and next to that a horsehair blanket, a gift from the seamstress. He didn't own much else besides pots, Dobson, and a '71 VW van. Packing wouldn't take long.

He pulled a duffle bag out of the closet and threw in some underwear and t-shirts. In a box on the closet shelf, he came across some old report cards his mother had sent him years before. They were from the Katherine of Sienna School outside Philadelphia. He remembered the time as anxious, hormone-driven years when he was taught a healthy respect for the backhand of a nun and how to diagram sentences. A talent for art earned him the task of decorating the schoolrooms for holidays. Basset hounds with green bow ties for St. Patrick's Day. That sort of thing. On a lark he applied for a scholarship and won a summer studying rope pottery with the Hopi Indians in northern Arizona. It was the first link in a life chain that had led him to Sturbridge. Until now he hadn't worried that might be the last.

Tomorrow he'd load a hundred or so pots from his shed into the van, and drive to Boston to raise cash. He went every summer. Visiting the galleries on Newbury Street. Contacting local collectors. Setting up the van in touristy Faneuil Hall.

He'd just be a little early this year.

———⟫●⟪———

Dobson pounded her left front hoof hard against the ground as if she understood what Seamus was saying and didn't like it. Seamus stroked her neck and whispered in her ear, "I promise." The mare shook her big grey and white head and turned away. Seamus walked slowly back to his van, took four pots from out back and handed them to his farmer friend as payment.

"She likes strawberries," Seamus reminded him.

He took the back roads, spirited by the signs of spring, and before long pulled onto Exit 9 of the Mass Pike. The entrance was backed up for over a mile. He finally reached the plaza where the tollbooths were being retrofitted with overhead cameras and reinforced with Jersey barriers. Signs of things to come.

It was warm for April in New England. He drove in

the slow lane so as not to endanger his cargo, nor challenge the old van's engine. Everyone seemed desperate to get home before the Interstates were closed, and minivans and RVs and sport utility crossovers jammed with kids and their pets, arms and legs sticking out from the blankets and bundles, their rooftops burdened with motorized gear, toboggans and skimobiles, furniture likely gathered up from second homes and destined for Craig's list roared by. The road was littered with what had been poorly secured. Mostly chunks of plastic so crushed by the on-rush of traffic their original purpose was no longer discernable.

Seamus dodged the flotsam and quietly cursed between taking reassuring deep breaths. Maybe the ban was a brilliant ploy after all, he thought. The perfect antidote to the meaningless rush; the idolization of motion; suspicion of anything at rest.

Wearily, he drove on.

As Boston drew near, he passed a billboard announcing that *Death of a Salesman* had been released as Death of a Salesman On Ice, coming soon to the Boston Garden. Another large colorful billboard invited everyone to the latest revival of Wild Bill's Traveling Wild West Show at the Convention Center. The ad featured someone he actually knew—Chosposi, chief of the Bear Clan, his sponsor and Hopi blood brother from a blissful summer as an apprentice potter. The once-proud Indian, a man of enormous quietness, stood before a Grand Cherokee SUV. Pinned on his chest was a bright orange button that read, "Ask Me About Our Nachos."

Seamus could think of little else for the rest of the ride into town.

Around him the eyes of passing drivers were filled with fear.

Chapter 11
I have a dream

For her descent into the city Carmen chose a clingy Missoni knit, a riotous yellow tam, open-toed sandals and Revo aviator sunglasses with purple lenses. She packed a dozen everyday outfits in a big steamer trunk—French skirts and scarves, hats from everywhere, t-shirts, cotton and linen tops, a cornucopia of accessories. She imagined an unbridled shopping spree up and down Boston's Newbury Promenade.

She glanced approvingly at her freshly painted toes and hurried downstairs to say good-bye to her father. As usual, she found him dozing in his office chair.

"You remember Dave?" he said, sensing her presence.

The horror of that terrifying day at MIT flooded over Carmen. She was in her early twenties, in Boston that Friday to drive her father home for a much-needed break at Wide Waters when jack-booted university police stormed into his lab. Instinctively, she had stepped between them and Bartholomew but was pushed roughly aside, and watched helplessly as her father was forced head first into a laboratory sink then bound from behind with plastic ties as if he was some package being readied for shipment. The police slapped locks on file cabinets, carelessly destroyed research projects, and took his lab assistant, Dave, away in cuffs. When they finally got back to Maine, Carmen promised her father she'd never leave his side. And there she'd remained busying herself in her uncle's boat business and seeing to Bartholomew's care.

Bartholomew saw her darken. "Dave's fine. In fact, we've been in touch. He'll contact you when you get to the city."

"So, the two of you are in cahoots again," Carmen said. "I should have guessed."

Bartholomew didn't tell her much. "Thought we might put a burr under the president's saddle," he said a little tentatively.

Carmen had guessed that much. She weighed taking on the White House and didn't like the odds. She had no particular love for North. He was an extension of the power structure that had humiliated her father. A fellow academic at that. Her father was likely using her to get even for this humiliation now, but Carmen was all right with that. It had been her humiliation, too. Besides, maybe it was her generation's turn, her turn, to pick up the gauntlet of civil disobedience.

"I'll make you proud," she promised him.

"You can handle it," Bartholomew said.

He was right.

Most people thought beauty always partnered with fragileness. That the prettiest among us fall out of warranty over the slightest thing. But Carmen had grit. She was a golden girl, true, but her childhood was rooted in nature. Her travels were encyclopedic and she learned early on to observe without prejudice and stand up for herself. She was at ease in unfamiliar surroundings and willing to explore her limits.

She leaned over and pressed her cheek hard against her father's. "No bourbon for breakfast," she admonished him. "Promise."

Then she left the house without looking back. Out front, she hopped into her packed-up Mazda sports coupe, dropped the manual shift into first gear and pressed down on the accelerator. She spun around the oval drive and tooted twice at Peppermint grazing in the lakefront pasture. Then she turned the sports car up the graceful serpentine entrance to Wide Waters and without braking turned right onto Rte. 302 toward Portland.

When she could, Carmen opened up the coupe, reveling in the sound of the engine's top end. Her long blond hair flew out behind her like an advertisement for fun. At exit 48, she got on the turnpike and headed south. She flashed under the Two Rod Road and over the Nonesuch River. Fifty minutes later she crossed over the wide mouth of the Piscataqua River and entered New Hampshire. She illegally used the free pass lane at the Hampton Toll Booth and roared into Massachusetts, picking up on the increased energy of the other drivers. She turned up the Eagles singing Desperado on her DVD player and left the sounds and smells of the country behind. She'd see her father again, and soon, she promised herself.

At last, just north of the city she caught her first glimpse of Boston's skyline. It sat on the ocean's edge like a giant amusement park.

———————>●<———————

Carmen exited the elevated highway at Storrow Drive and got off at Arlington Street. Turning onto Beacon she watched the numbers go by...five blocks later she pulled up in front of 346. The building was a red brick Queen Anne, four stories high, located on the river side, the sunny side, of the street. Carmen didn't know how long it had been unoccupied, but it looked in fine repair. The small fenced yard in front featured two glorious magnolia trees in full bloom. The front door was massive and carved in oak. The first floor windows were trimmed in stained glass and protected by bars. Altogether, it was just grand—a lifestyle Carmen was determined to revive.

The lock on the front door turned reluctantly. The hinges protested, too. As Carmen gave the door a final push, musty, cool air and perhaps a family ghost or two escaped. She tiptoed inside and said, "Hello," not as a question, but as a reverential greeting to the structure itself.

The central hall, which rose above her to the roof, housed the main staircase—a waterfall of deeply carved mahogany. A crystal chandelier hung above each stairway landing. There was a parlor to her left and to the right, etched-glass pocket doors revealed a long living room anchored by a pink marble fireplace flanked by gigantic oriental jars. She peeked around the corner. The living room led to a formal dining room in back. The furnishings throughout were dark and hand-embroidered. Everything was worn, but plush.

Carmen twirled herself into one of the floor-length velvet drapes. "Thank you, Uncle Brad," she said, dreamily.

She explored further. The kitchen was a mixture of French provincial and 1950's high tech. On the second floor, there was an art deco master suite complete with art deco tub. There were two more bedrooms on the third floor, and above that a huge open loft and smaller room that originally served as servants' quarters.

She climbed the last flight of stairs, to just below the great skylight that lit the entire home from within. She unlocked and pushed open the lead glass enclosure and climbed out. Before her lay a long-neglected but quixotic city garden filled with planters, elephant head benches and a rusty Victorian bird feeder. Sturdy evergreens that had weathered Boston's winters and years of inattention greeted her. A smattering of bulbs and hardy annuals survived in the planters and she picked a bunch of tulips. The garden was boxed in on either side by ivy-covered walls, and by the brownstone's mansard roof along the Beacon Street side. The effect was private, even cozy. The view was southwest, out over the Esplanade and across the widest part of the Charles River to the domes of MIT in Cambridge. Carmen snarled at them before she went back inside.

She left the flowers in the sink, went out to move her car around back into the double one-story garage and came back in through the kitchen entrance carrying the computers and small luggage. The rest could wait. She paraded through the house like a beauty queen bowing graciously to an audience of furniture and dozens of old paintings depicting buttoned-up people. Introducing herself to every unknown relative, she searched the cabinets and hutches and sideboards, but couldn't find a container for the flowers. She put them temporarily in an old mason jar she found in the pantry.

Finally, sitting down on the parlor settee and taking a deep satisfied breath, she said, "I need vases."

Chapter 12
Faster. Gentler.
Free shipping.

B ack in the 1960s, city planners in cahoots with commercial developers tore out the heart of Boston's rowdy nightlife district, then called Scollay Square. In its place, they planted an "upside down" building in the middle of a paved depression called City Hall Plaza. Upside down in architectural lingo meant that services used most often by the public were located on lower floors to ease access. Regarded by casual observers and experts alike as one of the country's most unfortunate examples of urban renewal, the building's drab cement exterior was a fair measure of what awaited citizens inside.

Peddler's Permits was on the 4th floor. The queue was short, likely the result of the impending travel ban, it occurred to Seamus. After a few minutes and $200 he was handed a big yellow sticker depicting a colonial cart vendor and the right to sell his wares in Faneuil Hall until Labor Day.

Back in his van, he eventually found a designated spot within sight of the main market and began unpacking his wares.

———————›»●‹‹———————

Carmen saw Seamus first. His shaggy flaxen hair, worn leather vest, and the rows of colorful pottery along the sides of the old van all caught her eye. She sashayed over.

"Your flower pots?" she asked.

Seamus, half asleep, didn't look up. "Yup," he said softly.

"They look Indian made."

"Indians taught me." He peeked up at Carmen. She was wearing a linen skirt that flowed in the breeze, ballet flats and tight fitting pink sweater. A fancy scarf was tied around her waist.

Carmen looked him over like he'd been caught for dinner. "Real Indians?" she asked with one raised eyebrow.

Seamus chuckled. "So you've heard about the fake Indians?" he said.

Carmen smiled but kept herself from laughing. "I like this one," she said, selecting a large azure blue vase encircled with tan diamond squares. "How much?"

"It's a set," Seamus replied, reaching down and handing her a matching vase in orange and green. "Two hundred for the pair," he said, thinking he might get quickly even on the permit fee.

"OK," Carmen said.

Who was this butterfly? he wondered.

Carmen walked around to the back of the van where

she noticed a horse harness and cans of leather cream laying in one corner. She came back around to the front, stood before Seamus and threw her weight onto one hip. "What's your horse's name?" she said.

They soon discovered they'd both been taught to ride horses by Indians and his was Dobson and hers was Peppermint. Seamus suggested they walk across the plaza to Regina's and get some pizza. They ate it back on the bench next to the bronze statue of Red Auerbach so Seamus could keep an eye on his van. They talked about horses all afternoon. They let the sound of songbirds and the reassuring spring sun wash over them.

Carmen didn't want to go home alone. She had promised her father she'd sit tight until Dave arrived, but surely he wouldn't object to such a handsome cowboy. A man whose strong-looking hands crafted such delicate art; a man who could tell first-person stories about real Indians. She bought more pots than she could carry. She fumbled with them in the old bags Seamus provided. She let out a little "oops."

Seamus was blinded by her freshness, the light that surrounded her. What were the odds of finding a pretty country girl in the middle of the city? "Hate to see you break those today," he said.

Carmen turned, smiled, and relaxed her shoulders. She was already imagining them in the big art deco bed.

Seamus delivered the pots and stayed for Chinese take-out. Carmen talked him into helping with the big steamer trunk still strapped on the back of the Mazda.

Up on the rooftop, they laughed and when he sensed

she was comfortable with his touch, Seamus kissed her.

"I'm a little new at this," she confessed.

Seamus had been wondering if he was going to have to sleep in the van.

"I'll go real slow," he promised her.

Chapter 13
Back from extinction

C armen was asleep beside him, curled up like a pretty pink snail, when a persistent knock on the front door woke Seamus up.

He rolled gently out of bed, pulled on his jeans and went downstairs.

When he opened the door, a tall angular man in a Red Sox cap constraining a mop of carrot-colored hair invited himself inside. "Who the hell are you?" the stranger asked, brushing by him.

"I spent the night," Seamus said. "Who the hell are you?"

The visitor looked Seamus over then yelled up the stairs, "Carmen!" Then to Seamus, "I'm the decorator."

Moments later Carmen leaned over the second floor railing then flew down the stairs and launched herself off the last step into the visitor's arms. He swung her round and round.

"Seamus McGuire," she called out on one pass, "meet Day-to-day Dave!"

Dave eventually put her down and hugged her for a

long time. He gave her a big sloppy great-to-see-you kiss on the cheek then whispered in her ear, "Sorry darling, but he has to go."

Chapter 14
Timing the market

After the staff had thinned out and the phones quieted down, they lit cigars on the second floor portico that looked over Constitution Mall. It was a crystalline evening. The Washington Monument looked like it might suddenly lift up and hop about.

Pipes Barronson was reviewing headlines with the president and chief of staff.

"The business community is getting its share of the dailies," he said. "We're better organized on radio and holding our own on the blogs. One thing we didn't see coming: average Joe and Jane don't seem to care. Our take is they're exhausted and that's working for us. People are rediscovering home life. Cutting the grass, planting flowers, repairing stuff, hanging in the park. This is one of our best storylines, takes in family values on one hand, and the sustainability crowd on the other."

"I like it," North said.

"We're buying time, Mr. President."

"Thanks, Pipes. Give us a best-of/worst-of going forward."

"Every morning, sir," Barronson said, getting up to leave.

When he was gone North turned to Wilkins who was smiling broadly.

"Sometimes you get the bear," Wilkins said.

"Ain't no money in the cure. Remember that?" North asked.

Wilkins nodded. "Chris Rock ragging on big pharma."

"Suppose our nasty little virus isn't really so bad? The deaths, sure—stop looking at me that way. I mean down the road."

"Things look a little bleak, now, Alex, but..."

"Listen...what do we need most?"

"A huge infusion of capital," Wilkins said.

"But without printing currency."

"That's the trick of it," Wilkins said.

"So who's got money?" North asked.

Wilkins turned his palms up to show they were empty.

"Tourists," North said. "The industry employs one in every seven people on the planet. Nothing's bigger bucks. Foreign tourists. Home-grown tourists. And what's our take? Some lousy national parks fees."

"Lose the summer season to a travel ban," Wilkins said, "and you've got an industry looking for a helping hand."

North took a long puff off his Honduran panatela. "Exactly," he said.

Chapter 15
Whistling a symphony

L ike the old friends they were, Dave and Carmen swung in the rooftop hammock in perfect rhythm. They'd been up since dawn. Around them, Boston was creaking to life. The traffic below on Storrow Drive was adding decibels. Rooftop pigeons were scratching around for early scraps. Dave was explaining what Bartholomew had in mind and how it was going to be.

"An online travelogue?" Carmen confirmed.

"Yup," said Dave.

"Using the old lecture tour movies?"

"Hosted by your avatar, yes."

"Because no one can travel?"

"Yup."

"Daddy thinks the president has something nefarious in mind, doesn't he?"

"The show will force his hand," Dave agreed.

"They'll come after us, guns blazing," Carmen said.

"Ummm," Dave said. "Your father was very concerned about that. He's been very resourceful. But to be safe, we can't leave here."

Carmen jumped up from the hammock. "Dammit. I knew there was something he wasn't sharing." She plopped back down.

They rocked in silence. An EVAC helicopter from Mass General passed overhead.

"I'm not even sure we should be up here during the day," Dave said. "Don't look up."

Carmen wondered what she'd gotten herself into. This wasn't just fighting City Hall; this was taking on the whole military-political-technology complex. Corrupt, power-mad, and presiding over a declining empire. The trifecta of unpredictability.

"I should have stayed home," she pined. "As a matter of fact, I haven't unpacked."

"Bartholomew is counting on us."

"Cell phones?" Carmen asked hopefully.

"Nope."

"Email?"

"Nope."

"Visitors?"

"Sorry."

She shuttered, then had a reassuring thought. "So Seamus stays."

"Not a chance."

"But we don't exist, right?'

"Afraid not."

"So who's going out for milk?" Carmen asked triumphantly.

———————

Dave went out the back door into the alley and took the plate number off Seamus' van. Up on the third floor where he had set up the Macs, he logged onto an unprotected wi-fi network and ran a search.

Retrieved: Seamus Thomas McGuire. Last known address: Sturbridge Village. Born: Philadelphia 1951. Raised Main Line. Penn State '72 on a ROTC scholarship. Discharged from the regular Army after four years. Routine decorations cited. Minimal health records. Pennsylvania and Massachusetts drivers' licenses. No rap sheet. Pictures: championship track in high school and at State. No siblings. Parents deceased.

Dave dug deeper and came across a cache of news clippings documenting Seamus' professional career as a pot maker. His grant to study with the Hopi Indians. The creation of a pottery museum at the Grand Canyon in which he played a supporting role. Then his appointment to Sturbridge Village as master potter. The record-setting sale of his wares during a PBS fundraiser.

It all seemed straightforward until Dave ran a chronology. Fifteen years ago, the data stopped. Not a single record between then and when Seamus showed up at Sturbridge five years later.

What was he doing? ROTC and pottery—how do you dress for that?

Carmen appeared in the doorway. She was hunting for a place to put Seamus' vases that now overflowed with tulips.

Dave gave her the news.

"Maybe he didn't have a real address. Maybe he

was living in his truck?" she said.

"I've watched him. He does things with a easy confidence," Dave said. "Not the kind of training you get in art school."

"He knows horses. I trust him."

"Jesus, Carmen. Are you ass over tea-kettle already?"

"Hasn't Daddy already seen to that?"

Dave backed off.

"Overseas, maybe?" Carmen offered.

"Only two ways to leave the data stream," Dave said. "Feds and felons."

"I'll keep an especially close eye on him," Carmen said. "Just in case he's a Fed."

Dave realized how disappointed she was at not being able to enjoy a public life in Boston. Even with her loyalty to Bartholomew, he knew darn well sooner or later she'd get restless. She was right, too—her father's scheme was ambitious and if they were successful, it'd be 24/7. Somebody had to keep the house running. Bartholomew wouldn't like it, but he didn't have to know. Besides, keeping Seamus might come in handy—especially if things turned sour.

Carmen put the vases on a wall shelf behind Dave, came up behind him and rubbed his shoulders. She watched as his hands danced across the keyboard, screens and databases flashing by. He played a computer like a Steinway.

The unexpected by-product of a liaison between a motel operator and a Christian missionary, Dave had been raised instead by Gnostic in-laws who cycled him through religious schools and computer camps. Isolated, he discovered the Internet when it was still being developed by DARPA. In junior high he took on small hacking jobs for friends. And for spending money. He earned a reputation for being able to find things, especially people, and the word spread. By the time he entered MIT he counted both the underground and several little-known federal agencies among his clients. For a freshman project, he launched an on-line novelty store. His flavored communion wafers were a big hit. As was the first Swiss army knife for gays. It featured a lemon zester.

It was enterprise and this twisted irreverence that caught Professor Bartholomew Brand's eye. He hired Dave as his assistant at the university's New Media Lab and treated him like a son.

Dave shut the Mac down. The missing block of time in Seamus' background was suspicious. He needed more time to figure out who their houseguest really was.

"What even makes you think he'll stay?" he asked Carmen.

"Davie!" Carmen vogued. "Haven't you taken one good look at me?"

Chapter 16
Nothing is more important than human life. Oil.

The medical chief of Health and Human Services, a tiny dark-haired woman who blinked constantly behind her over-sized reading glasses, addressed in serious tones the Emergency Team assembled in the Oval Office.

"We're calling it Born-1 because it's from Borneo and it's the first of its kind," she said. "Like most viruses this one infects healthy cells by teaching them to produce virus cells. But this one does it at the rate of four million per hour. That's fast enough to overwhelm immune systems, which explains the near-instant deaths. We haven't been able to establish a thread between the San Diego event and the two outbreaks in Chicago and Boston. Routine flights, separate airlines. No family or business relations. Different origination points. Different crews. We're scrubbing these lists six ways to Sunday, but we're not on top of it yet, Mr. President."

North stared at the grim faces around the room. "Still no incidents overseas?" he asked.

"No sir," the chief of staff replied. "Not one."

"Muslim virus," Pipes said.

Everybody stared at him.

"I'm serious," he said.

"We're paying hell for closing our air space," the transportation secretary said. "Was a lot easier after 9/11."

North looked around the room. "Are we to believe that we have simultaneous, independent sources in three cities for the same disease?" he said.

"We don't believe that, Mr. President," the CDC representative said.

Darsk, the head of the National Security Agency who'd been asked to join the team, spoke up. "I agree, sir. There's simply no way to know whether this is a fluke, or the beginning of a series of incidents. It's possible, just possible, that we're under attack."

"Bio-invasion?"

"Let's not take it off the table, sir," said Darsk.

"OK, let's not," the president agreed.

Chapter 17
Friendly fire

Alexander North was an imposing man before becoming president. A respected teacher and author, he was also a natural athlete and moved with a grace that suggested gallantry. This made his adversaries, political and otherwise, pause. Plus it made women swoon. He squinted in that western way which suggested deep thinking and expansive answers. He stood six-foot-three beneath wavy black hair just graying at the temples, and sported outsized chocolate brown eyes that glowed with sincerity whenever a voter or camera came near.

Alexander had followed his father into the Arizona governors' mansion several years earlier. Big Bo North had built a reputation for toughness by assembling a law-enforcement organization second in foregone conclusions only to the Iraqi penal code. Within 18 months of taking office, he had wiped the state clean of rustlers, vagrants, kidnappers, deadbeats, assorted bushwhackers and illegal immigrants by imprisoning hundreds and executing several dozen. Alexander inherited a state operating in the black, monies he re-directed into infrastructure, education and water, all the while keeping Arizona debt-free by closing down do-nothing agencies, slashing state employee benefits and outsourcing services. When he accepted the University of Northern Arizona's offer to become the school's chancellor after just one term, most of his supporters thought he no longer yearned for a national stage.

He did have enemies. His critics warned he was vain and power-drunk, but many more argued he was that rare leader who understood how to make government work for regular folk. He encouraged this latter view by campaigning for president in a white hat, dusty jeans and snakeskin boots. He loved animals, the land, and sang a fair baritone. He shared his straightforward opinions with refreshing candor and surprising empathy. The electorate loved his all-American profile and was comforted by his gentle humanism.

Alexander wasn't just all hat. He had cattle, too.

It was as if Ronald Reagan had gone to Yale.

Ten days after the San Diego outbreak, the virus had spread to six locales. Three hundred and seventy-five people were infected. The death rate was a scary fifty percent and there was no vaccine in sight. There was a lot of grousing about the ban's inconvenience, but no sign of a popular revolt. Only a handful of people knew about the country's looming financial collapse—and not one of them wanted their name associated with breaking the news.

Disease and default had completely consumed

North's waking hours. He eventually recognized them as one problem and that was key. He came to see that one was the reason for and the other the justification for the strategy that had finally taken shape in his mind.

———————

Most Americans knew Mary Morningstar as a former Ms. Arizona. A second title, that of Ms. Navaho Nation, the honor she was more proud of, was largely unknown outside the 250,000 surviving members of her tribe. That crown was won in an exhausting contest that involved dancing, quick thinking and feats of strength including shearing an uncooperative sheep. She had cinched the title Ms. Arizona by correctly answering questions about television programs in a bathing suit.

Mary Morningstar was also a former student in Professor Alexander North's course on the American West. She had gone on to law school afterwards, then built a successful practice helping native tribes build and operate gambling casinos. The statuesque, doe-eyed 37-year-old was an early and popular appointee to North's cabinet.

"Nice to see you, Mr. President," she greeted him later that morning. They met in the cozy blue room next to the Oval Office where treaties were often signed.

"Our travel industry is in for a tremendous beating," North said, motioning for her to sit. "Coffee, Madam Secretary?"

She shook her head.

"I want the government to intervene. Specifically,

your department."

"Anything Commerce can do, Mr. President."

The president labeled his idea the National Infrastructure Forum, or NIF. It served as a model for how certain government offices would operate in the future, and it said nothing about tourism. In reality, it was a real estate investment trust with a government-backed guarantee. The guarantee came in the form of insurance with a hair-trigger buy-out clause. If it turned out to be a particularly bad year for tourism in the United States, something North was counting on, the federal government would end up owning a big chunk of the industry.

"Well, we're not going to bail out Las Vegas," the president said laughing.

Mary laughed, too. "If I understand you, what would the government want with thousands of failed businesses?" she asked. "Especially at a time like this?"

"At a time like what?" North asked slowly.

"I mean to say, tough economic times, sir."

"We're already in the travel business," North said, smiling again. "We host 400 million visitors every year in our national parks alone. We designate high-profile historic sites. Like Graceland, as you know."

"We're not the most visited country in the world," Ms. Morningstar said. "We're second behind France."

"True," North agreed. "But the point is, we can be first. Commerce needs to get more involved. Move quietly and keep it inside your office," North instructed her. "The chief of staff will provide a legal pathway and he can smooth over any issues."

"The ban will be over soon?" the secretary asked, getting up from her own chair as the president rose.

"We're all hoping for that," North said, draping his arm across her shoulders and showing her out.

Chapter 18
Certain informational advantages

They were downstairs lounging on the carved Victorian couch across from the big pink fireplace flanked by the giant spice jars. Carmen's head rested on Seamus' lap, her bare feet rested on the sofa arm. She was twirling a daisy between her fingers.

"Davie thinks you're a spy," she said.

"I am," Seamus said mischievously.

"Who are you spying on?"

Seamus grinned. He tapped Carmen on the nose and moved his finger tip down to trace her lips. "Why, you, Carmen."

"Me?" Carmen said. "Heavens, why me?"

"Doesn't Day-to-day Dave know?" Seamus' finger fell from her chin and slid down her neck.

"He thinks I should be afraid."

Seamus' finger stopped at the top of her breastplate and Carmen felt a slight pressure.

"Are you?" he said.

"No."

"Good." Seamus kissed her forehead and then laced

the fingers of one hand with hers. "There's nothing to be afraid of."

"Has anyone but me bought a pot?"

Seamus hesitated. "Actually, no. In fact, I was thinking it was getting time for me to get back to Faneuil Hall. And Sturbridge before they close the highways."

"Davey will come around," Carmen said trying to sound confident.

"Doesn't figure into it."

Carmen arched her back, and looked up to meet his eyes. "Suppose I give you a job?" she said.

"Doing what?"

"Building stuff. Help me fix up the place. Put in a broadcast studio, actually. I'm thinking of doing a yoga thing online."

"You and Andy Hardy Dave are going to put on a play?"

"You might say."

Seamus second-guessed his exit plan. Had he fallen in love? Had she? Love or lust, no telling which in springtime. And no telling when the Village would reopen.

"My horse is...."

"I have a barn, I can help with that."

Seamus clasped her hands firmly in his and the daisy stopped twirling. "Why doesn't Dave trust me?" he said.

"He doesn't like your pots," Carmen said. "Wouldn't decorate with them."

Seamus chuckled, then he leaned back, and let the unexpected invitation find a comfortable place in his mind. After a moment, he looked down to ask her why she hadn't wanted to walk down the Esplanade earlier. For that matter, why Dave didn't go out at all. But Carmen, feeling safe, had fallen asleep.

Chapter 19
Shiny happy people

Carmen handed Seamus a fistful of cash to run errands all over town. He returned with the van loaded. After hauling everything to the third floor, he started knocking two-by-fours together. He soundproofed the wall on the Beacon Street side of the room, then installed three pairs of Bose speakers and added a woofer under the platform he'd built as a stage. Over the next couple of days he re-plastered one wall Dave wanted to use as a green screen, installed overhead lights, and fitted the windows with blackout shades.

"Stage is a little small," Carmen chided him.

"Much bigger than your yoga mat," Seamus said.

"I fibbed about that. More like a travel show."

"Just when no one can travel?" Seamus mused.

"OK, smarty-pants, an underground travel show." Carmen winked at him as if to form a pact.

Carmen busied herself with the tedious task of cataloging the film from her childhood tours into a useful database. She cross-referenced by location, attractions, run time and mood. She recorded any notes and anecdotes she could recall. She also took on the job of collecting clippings and video snippets her avatar would use for commentary on future shows. These, too, went into the database.

One afternoon, the cameras and sound equipment Dave had ordered were delivered. He set up the studio for 3D, and in a trial run pasted wireless sensors all over Carmen's body. As she moved around on camera, her avatar, Bartholomew's brilliant invention, moved around on screen with the same natural grace and ease. The camera loved Carmen and she felt safe under the warm lights. She practiced her broadcast voice and Dave texture-mapped the digital version to replicate it perfectly.

Dave then dedicated himself to making the avatar's face just like Carmen's. Building on Bartholomew's software, he started with an articulated wire frame to present her countenance then used old family photos of Carmen to precisely capture every nuance and expression. He worked late into the night, Carmen occasionally getting out of bed to bring him snacks and water.

"So folks won't be able to tell the difference between Carmen and her avatar?" Seamus asked Dave one morning.

Seamus was surprised by Dave's response. "What were you doing before Sturbridge?" Dave asked.

Seamus was caught short. Surely Dave had investigated him. What did he know? Not enough if he was still digging around.

"I was blood brother to the Hopi."

"Living on their reservation?

"Yes—in northern Arizona."

"Not much up there."

"Even the coyotes are lonely," Seamus said.

"What did Carmen tell you?" Dave asked.

"She told me about the raid on the New Media Lab."

"'Nuff said," Dave replied.

"I'd like to know one other thing," Seamus said, watching Dave manipulate images on the screen. Amazed at how interchangeable Carmen and her on-screen duplicate already were.

"What's that?" Dave said.

"How long before Carmen can't tell the difference between that avatar and herself?" Seamus asked.

———⤞●⤝———

It took them three weeks. Just before Memorial Day weekend, Dave announced they were ready.

They met in the third floor studio for a preview. Seamus arrived first with a beer in one hand, followed by Carmen carrying trail mix and champagne. She wore silver sneakers and a long purple t-shirt cinched at the waste by a braided silver rope. Her hair was up in big banana curls that danced around her ears. She looked like Helen of Troy had gotten ready for Dancing With the Stars.

"I wish Daddy were here," Carmen said settling into one of the new beanbag chairs.

"Speech," Seamus said to Dave, plopping down on a beanbag himself.

"To our beloved President, Alexander North," Dave said raising the glass of champagne Carmen had poured, "a colonoscopy of epic proportions, a perverse proctologist armed with an endless sigmoidoscope. May it enter painfully, grow thick and have babies."

They drank lustily and Carmen refilled the glasses.

"To my father," she said. "And to his spiritual guide, Gandhi."

They emptied their glasses again. Dave bowed ceremoniously before Carmen. "You have captured the beauty of the universe and placed it on our doorstep."

Carmen applauded.

Dave spun around and with a great flourish collapsed back into the last beanbag and pushed the clicker. "Watch out for this," he said.

The monitor came to life. The show's opening sequence was kaleidoscopic, accompanied by the driving beat of native drums. Icons and images gushed from the screen.

Carmen and Seamus were pressed into their seats by the energy.

Casaba Rendor's archival tapes filled the background like wallpaper. Carmen, as a lithe and winsome teenager, climbed over the ruins at Troy, ran along the ocean's edge on Normandy's beaches, peeked out from under a pith helmet somewhere deep in the jungle.

Seamus leaned forward when he realized these were images of Carmen as a jaunty teenager. As she moved from venue to venue, the database symbolically linked to the old film spewed forth the iconography of each locale. Dave had mixed in heuristics, symbolic analysis, visual mapping techniques, the latest in neurosilicon chips.

He had art directed a stew that could think.

Then without warning, in extreme close-up, Carmen's avatar suddenly appeared.

Lips moist.

"Where in the world is Digital Darling?" the look-alike said.

You could see halfway down her throat.

Seamus couldn't take his eyes off the screen. Bold and gutsy, he admitted to himself. Perhaps he'd under-estimated both of them. Maybe this little escapade was going to create a fuss after all.

"More champagne!" Carmen screamed, heading for the kitchen.

A triumphant toast was raised.

And another.

It was time to rattle reality.

Chapter 20
Babe alert!

The Digital Darling Show debuted on Friday evening of Memorial Day weekend. Just as Bartholomew had predicted, the signal rode the omnipresent hum of the inter-networked world and appeared without warning on screens large and small. On big plasma TVs in sports bars and on handhelds, iPhones and BlackBerries. It interrupted conversations, police scanners, news shows and medical operations.

Dave had created what Bartholomew had imagined: an intoxicating travelogue hosted by an aware and pre-scient host. As Carmen spoke and moved around the studio on camera, Digital Darling spoke and moved on screen. As Carmen's avatar changed subjects, the system retrieved clips from the database that reflected what she was saying.

The audience was seduced and taken for a roller coaster ride at the same time. On some magical mystery tour held together by an underlying visual logic, the relentless beat of the drums and most of all, by Digital Darling's unclear intentions. She was methamphetaminic, but under control.

The broadcast amused millions and impressed experts. Within days, NetQuote awarded the personage Digital Darling the highest Q-quotient ever recorded by a broadcast personality. She was the most likeable host in the history of mass media. The mysterious holiday weekend broadcast was attributed to gods, aliens and Chinese hackers in that order.

Just who was this unfettered imp? This sex-tinged waif cast to the four corners of the world at the moment of her true innocence. Who had sponsored this irresistible invitation to adventure? To the awaiting joys of travel? And just who was Digital Darling? A precocious middle-aged hipster through whose eyes the mysteries of culture unfolded in rapid fire. She beckoned. She made you want to get up and go. And she raised provocative questions about the wisdom of a ban on travel.

Before long everyone wanted to know more.

Including, of course, North's inner circle.

Chapter 21
Deregulation

As usual Francis Darsk, the NSA director, was nervous. He rubbed his nose with his fist, a habit he picked up as a boxer in the Marines.

He glanced up from the laptop on the president's desk.

The chief of staff and Pipes Barronson looked up, too.

"Is the young girl real?" North asked.

"The teenager version is, yes," Darsk said. "The lab scanned every frame. The cars and signage—it was all shot in the 1970s and '80s."

The four men stared at the screen.

"The Elvis Is Alive Museum is relocating to Tupelo, Mississippi," Digital Darling said. "And parents take note. Some Japanese cartoons are capable of causing seizures—don't leave the kids in front of the TV over there. Thinking closer to home? Try San Francisco. Bus tours of the infamous Haight-Ashbury district point out highlights of the neighborhood made famous by hippies and music. Tours also explain the language and customs of the hippies."

Iconic baby boomer band posters from Fillmore West popped up around her avatar's shoulders.

"Is she a real person?" Barronson asked.

"We're working that," Darsk said. "The image is digitally created, but her expressions, the subtleties, and of course the fact that she appears to be talking extemporarily suggests she's human."

"She's the one in the old film?" North said.

"That's our guess. We're running a special program on the young girl's face—see if it ages accordingly. Course it could be her twin sister. Or maybe the author came across the old footage and used it to create his own more mature version."

North tried to be patient. "Her. It. What do we know for sure, Frank?"

"We know this, Mr. President. The broadcast doesn't have a particular source. It's always there, roaming around in bits that assemble randomly to build the show. It's been online three times now. We're working on a trace, of course, but it's a big world."

"Pops up out of nowhere?" Wilkins said skeptically "And it's everywhere?"

"It's possible, I'm told," Darsk said. "At least mathematically."

"Meanwhile, we can't block it, unscramble it, can't even find it?" North didn't need the questions answered.

"Try knocking out a few computers," the chief of staff suggested.

"We thought of that. Our people don't think it'll

work," Darsk said. "Creates a hell of an uproar, too."

"We don't like uproars," Barronson said, figuring that the mess would end up on his desk.

"Just need a little time, Mr. President," Darsk said. "I've got two Crays crunching nothing but this. We'll find her, I promise you. There's a pattern buried in there somewhere."

Frustrated, North ended the meeting. After the NSA director and Barronson left, he turned to his chief of staff.

"Couldn't find two balls in a locker room," the president said.

His chief of staff tapped his cigar into an ashtray Ulysses Grant once used. "We used to be such good spies," he said wistfully.

"This show is a monkey wrench."

"Maybe we should bring in someone new?" Wilkins suggested.

"Who we got?"

"Cyber Defense Academy. Computer Emergency Response Team…"

"How about somebody brand new?" North suggested. "Our own man."

"Hmm," Wilkins said, warming to the idea. "Somebody rogue."

Part Two

"Without your applause,
I do not exist."
– Stephen Colbert

Second interrogation
In defense of WikiLeaks

On the third day of questioning, the interrogator sitting across from Seamus slammed his hand down hard on the table. "You're guilty, McGuire. You knew from the beginning."

"Knew what?" Seamus asked with a smirk. He swung one leg over the corner of the table. "A gay hacker and his country sidekick were going to topple the empire? We all that delicate?"

"When some digital concoction functions like a real person, the folks in charge get testy."

"If something came of it, I was already on the inside," Seamus argued. "What more could the agency want?'"

"You went over."

"Prove it."

The interrogator got up from his side of the table and paced around the inside perimeter of the small room as if he were trapped there, too. He brushed back his crew cut with one hand then, back at Seamus, "What we require at this time, Mr. McGuire, is confidence about which side you're on. The side of those willing to give their government the benefit of the doubt? Or the side that thinks undermining their president is *goddam patriotic!"*

Just think, Seamus thought to himself. If I'd stayed active I could spend every day with people like this. "Protest is only treason when you lose," he said.

"Don't hand me any John Brown crap about putting the ruling class on their ass. Ain't worth a shit if you're not standing in the middle of something called a country."

"I get it. I got it before."

"Be best if that was a kick-ass country!"

"I get that, too. What was I supposed to do? Leave her to that crazy Mexican?"

"What Mexican?" the government man said, finally sitting back down.

"Poncho."

"Never heard of him."

"Agent Poncho," Seamus said, pointing to the paperwork on the table.

"Again, not in the file."

Seamus slumped into his chair.

It was the interrogator's turn to smirk.

Chapter 22
How to make money
without lifting things

Poncho's earliest memory was that of flying. At age two he was tossed over the steel fence that guarded the Mexican/U.S. border. He was headed north, one of about 800 immigrants who every night successfully challenged the ill-kept ramparts. That night his mother spent hours crawling through the gullies, washes and storm culverts that crisscrossed the no-man's land just north of Nogales. She carried him papoose style, once diving into a sewage drain to avoid the vigilante searchlights and the feared ATF helicopters. She almost smothered him and he never got the stink out of his nose.

He grew up in the San Fernando Valley on the poor side of Burbank. By age ten, he could pick the pocket of a cop on duty. At thirteen, he carried a Glock. At nineteen, going nowhere, he took a job as a movie double with a company called Warriors. They trained Hollywood actors for combat roles. They made famous people dig foxholes and live in them. They set off real explosions and used live ammunition. They made women cry and grown men cry out.

Poncho signed on as an airman, someone who stepped onto concealed launching ramps rigged with explosives that propelled him toward the camera as a bomb went off behind. He built a career by volunteering for the most dangerous stunts.

After seven years he could still pass for Antonio Banderas at a distance, but he was deaf in one ear, nursed a slight limp, and had had enough. He set his horizons between what the son of an illegal immigrant might reasonably expect, and what was possible in a land where the Constitution read like a travel brochure. He grew a mustache, bought a fiery red Continental convertible and headed east. He ended up in Boston where he took a room at the Copley Hotel because they didn't ask a lot of questions if you paid in cash.

One morning, about a week in town, he was sitting on a park bench in the Commonwealth Avenue mall reading the *Sunday Globe*. A classified ad headlined "Got Nerve?" caught his eye. Downtown on Monday he found a door temporarily labeled *Interviews* on the tenth floor of the JFK Building.

"Poncho? Just Poncho?" the interviewer began. I need two names. First and last."

"Mr. Poncho," Poncho said.

The interviewer grimaced and moved down the application form.

"Everybody has a social security number," he said, getting ready to write.

Poncho smiled at him. Lost amid the palm trees and power lines of Los Angeles, he had never registered for anything, not school, not the army, not even for a checking account.

The interviewer scribbled in the margin. "What do you know about the U.S. Constitution?"

"Floating in the harbor."

"The *document*."

Poncho flashed his trademarked toothy grin. "Pretty sure you mean the boat, senor."

The interviewer used the other margin. "Formal education?" he asked next.

"Pre-law," Poncho said without blinking. His mother had allowed no Spanish to be spoken in the house, so he had learned English and not a few things about the American legal system by watching *The People's Court* and *Judge Judy*. The law fascinated him.

"Please answer the following questions Yes or No. Does the government have your federal 1040 tax form on file?"

"No."

"Are you a citizen?"

"No."

"Have you ever been charged with a crime?"

"Misdemeanor? Felony?"

"That's a 'Yes.' Are you in good physical condition?"

Poncho opened his shirt. His muscular body was smattered with scars.

The instructor stared nervously, then made additional notes on the back of the form.

"Do you feel the laws of the United States apply to others, but not to you?"

Poncho leaned forward his eyes laughing. "Doesn't everybody, my friend?"

"I need to photocopy your driver's license."

"Already a copy."

The government agent groaned. "Will you provide names—former employers, relatives—as references?"

Poncho cocked his head. "People you gonna ask questions?"

Over the next few days the government interviewed some 200 candidates. Not one, it seemed, was more qualified than this enigmatic Mexican from the west coast who, an exhaustive investigation revealed, had spent over three decades in the United States without ever signing his real name.

The job was for deep cover work.

"This guy already doesn't exist," said Chief of Staff Wilkins at a national security meeting later, sealing the deal.

Chapter 23
Can you hear me now?

The growing popularity of *The Digital Darling Show* galled Darsk and he needed to thwart the momentum. He authorized a private task force inside the National Security Agency. At the first meeting with his staff, he put Priority One in unmistakable terms, "Find that bitch."

Scores of administrators were soon keeping tabs on dozens of field agents who were tracking down hundreds of leads. Darsk "borrowed" many of the government's best hackers, and brought some to Forte Meade to work in teams. They were a ragamuffin bunch of kids living on energy water, Ritalin and HotPockets. They took over an empty hanger and filled it with whiteboards that were quickly filled with competing algorithms. Several became contributors to blogs and chat rooms discussing Digital Darling.

Despite a 24/7 effort, the NSA director had trouble staying ahead of the gathering Digital Darling storm. Not one hacker on his staff had a clue about how a signal could ride on the hum of a network. Or, a promising notion about how to find its source.

"How come the cleverest minds liked being criminals?" Darsk grumbled to anyone who would listen.

Back in D.C., Pipes Barronson's publicity factory took over another floor in the Eisenhower Building. The mission was to keep up a continuous counter-narrative on the importance of honoring the travel ban—and the horrific consequences of ignoring it. Each time someone caught the flu, a concerned federal government asked if this was the start of the Pandemic Outbreak.

Television was a problem for the White House. Speculation about exactly where Digital Darling was hiding was constant. Real or not, she was beautiful, sexy and elusive—so every host, anchor and wag had something to say. Carmen groupies formed fan clubs and strove to be more like her. They got airtime. The tabloids fed the verbal frenzy with headlines questioning her origins, referencing everything from secret bio/silicon experiments to UFOs. Then came a two-hour Science Channel special on artificial life forms delving into her digital genome. The blogosphere blew the discussion wide open branching into First Amendment rights, romantic patriotism, the nature of reality, and of course, ownership and control of the Internet. Social media kept the precious woman/ child top of mind everywhere from the halls of Congress to the nation's sparsely populated beaches.

Digital Darling herself fueled the debate; ending every show in some exotic locale with the provocative question, "Wish you were here?"

Public appetite for the e-mystery shocked even grizzled media veterans.

On Beacon Street, the trio worked hard to keep the government on its heels. By late June, they were putting out four half-hour shows every day. But the appetite for content was insatiable and they were growing weary from no respite nor exercise, and nauseous from too much MSG in the Thai takeout.

Dave sent out spiders to do some dirty work. They flooded government computers with e-cards picturing the world's most desirable destinations. Sympathetic copycats issued millions more and occasionally brought down the NSA's networks.

In the studio, Carmen experimented with more movement. She moved first to the edge of the stage and then to the four corners of the studio. One day she wore a body stocking and Digital Darling appeared as a fantasy in silhouette. Dave had handed her two daisies to use as a prop and she twirled them thoughtfully between her fingers.

"I could be in the Grand Canyon," she said, pulling off one pedal. "I could be staring at the Statue of Liberty. Or I might not be here at all. Maybe you have learned to blend real and virtual experiences and the difference between them is no longer interesting. Just where are you at?"

With that question the database offered up hundreds of psychedelic album covers from the '60s.

Her Q-Score climbed relentlessly higher. The driving

native drums never stopped, a relentless reminder that you, gentle viewer, weren't going anywhere.

Seamus moved into research. The more he tracked the public discourse, the more he found himself leaning toward a more strident commentary. An evermore condemning prophesy. He fed Carmen show themes like the Dennis Hopper quote, *Our inheritance is freedom*, which Carmen brought to life with first hand memories of her overseas adventures as the database presented moments from history when governments had failed to squelch individual initiative.

As Seamus urged Carmen to make Digital Darling more immediate, Dave gave the show more context. For one show, he moved her out of the studio and filmed her sweeping down the brownstone's magnificent carved stairway like Scarlet O'Hara. One night they filmed the show in low light in the roof garden and ran Moody Blues music behind an ephemeral Digital Darling. A second ghost-like presence, the teenaged Carmen, explored famous haunts like Gettysburg and the endless fields of white crosses at Normandy.

It drove Darsk nutty.

As the nation's birthday weekend approached, the White House held its breath. It was ground zero in a country that wasn't taking a summer vacation. Across the land, plenty of folks were calling for North's neck, but so far behind closed doors. Most people still gave him the benefit of the doubt. The polls revealed that the general public overwhelmingly favored his better safe than sorry strategy, and even better believed that the president dearly loved his country.

Nevertheless the underground trio wasn't celebrating. Dave understood from the mounting number of probes in search of their location, Carmen Brand was now the most wanted woman in America.

Chapter 24
A digital drift net

North met his commerce secretary in the rose garden. They sat under a big red white and blue umbrella overlooking Independence Mall. The secret service was out of earshot.

"We already have 27 percent of the nation's tourism industry under contract," Ms. Navaho said softly. "We're adding two points a week. Most simply couldn't survive a lost season so we picked them up easily. Others, I'm happy to report, cooperated out of loyalty to the country, and to you personally. Some decided to sell now, assuming that things were just going to get worse. Some, of course, just needed the money. Frankly, the momentum has been terrific, Mr. President."

North could scarcely refrain from throwing her a high five.

"Give me the hard bark, too," he said.

"Well, not everyone is onboard," Ms. Navaho admitted. "The gay community has taken a portion of the industry underground. We estimate this is substantial, maybe 15 percent. The overall black market is difficult to measure but services like chartered transportation and concierge assistance are clearly thriving."

"Excellent," North congratulated her. "What about Disney?"

The secretary blushed. "They said the NSA's ears are already too big."

"We sent a team down there?"

"Yes sir. They gave our agents free passes good for a year. And big Mickey ears."

"Christ," North uttered. "We're getting pistol whipped by Mouseketeers."

"I'm working the problem, Mr. President. You could do something for me. The feedback from Wall Street is taking on a threatening tone."

"Tough to do anything quietly in this town," North said with a smile. "Leave Wall Street to me. Pipes is on that. You're doing great work on Main Street. This is bigger than you think and you're at the center of it."

He took her hand. "Keep your own counsel. And keep on buying, that is, insuring."

The secretary thanked the president and made her way across the south lawn.

North lingered for a few moments, staring off at the Jefferson Memorial and wondering if his predecessor would approve. Either way, he was damned if he was going to preside over national bankruptcy. Go down in history as the man who destroyed the American Dream. Who's kidding whom? Wanting more than your share of the pie was the American Dream.

It had been a good week; the pieces were falling

into place. He decided he would leave Washington early
this Friday. Maybe spend some time up at Camp David.
Couldn't call that a vacation, exactly.

Chapter 25
Poseurs

Seamus went out to buy steaks. He would grill them on the hibachi he'd set in the roof garden over the weekend. He cut across the Public Gardens and made his way to a small grocery store on Newbury Street. It was a real summer day. Folks lying on every available patch of grass getting sun, air conditioners whirling away in windows, the Red Sox playing the Yankees at Fenway Park.

As he walked along, Seamus was surprised to find so many storefront displays filled with Digital Darling paraphernalia. Cosmetic and clothing lines, bottled water and power drinks, and a line of imported wines all claimed official status. Digital Darling hats, scarves, leotards and ballet shoes. At the corner of Dartmouth Street the new DD Travel Boutique was Coming Soon.

Some retailers had also placed monitors in their windows with editions of *The Digital Darling Show* playing on endless loop. Seamus paused outside one store long enough to watch young Carmen scamper from cabana to mountain pass, from hotel lobby to remote outpost on her whirlwind journey of discovery—journeys many people no longer imagined for themselves.

What Seamus saw next stopped him in his tracks.

Three women strutted arm-in-arm down the famous promenade toward him.

They were dead ringers for Digital Darling.

———————⟹⊳●⊲⟸———————

Back home Seamus found Carmen emerging from the tub in the art deco bathroom. She greeted him with a soft smile. He came up behind her, slowly unwrapped her towel.

"We can do this nice and easy," he said, "or we can do it nice and rough."

Carmen shivered, then whispered, "Nice and rough."

He guided her to the bed and at first touched her gently. He warmed his hands with the orange-scented lotion she kept on her nightstand and worked it into her back, then her legs and arms. He played with the peach fuzz at the small of her back until she moaned. He traced the meridians of her nervous system in the lotion then pushed his thumbs down hard at major cross points. Carmen arched up slightly at the initial pain but then sank deeply into the bed as the tension in her body flowed away.

Seamus rolled her over and played with her nipples until they were as hard as he was. Then he lifted her to her knees, spanked her playfully and took her from behind until at last they both collapsed.

They dozed in each other's arms for the rest of that

afternoon. Their war against the government couldn't have seemed farther away.

"I saw women on the street today that looked exactly like you," he said at one point.

"My poseurs," Carmen said dreamily.

Around seven Dave knocked on the bedroom door to talk about what they wanted on their pizza.

Chapter 26
Mr. Smith goes to Washington

Just before the Legislature took its regular August break, President North called for the first joint session of Congress to be held off Capitol Hill since the War of 1812. He invited the distinguished members of both Houses to join him at the Kennedy Center for the Performing Arts, the triumphant white marble complex that sat a mile away on the far side of the Potomac River.

It was Pipes' idea. Both the off-campus venue and the occasion: a rare mid-year State of the Union Address.

"Get them off the Hill where they feel invincible," Pipes advised. And that night they straggled in, late, complaining about being so far from their food-delivery services and mistresses.

The president also appreciated Pipes' stagecraft. Three enormous movie screens formed a backdrop behind the podium where he would speak. His communications director had also made a movie for the occasion. It was comprised largely of people writhing in agony, grieving bedside relatives, dismembered children, piled up corpses, stomach turning displays of bodies ravaged by disease. Nearly every frame was seeped in bodily fluids. Barronson later conceded that he had thrown in a few car accident victims for effect, and the resulting on-screen carnage was worth the risk—at its best, almost unwatchable. It ended with never-before-seen footage of the mad panic inside Terminal B at San Diego's Lindbergh Field.

Wall Street had been invited, too. Barronson seated them in the front rows of the grand auditorium where, if everything went according to plan, they would become the president's most enthusiastic cheerleaders.

Eventually the House Speaker called them all to order and the unusual session got underway. The room darkened as President North was introduced. The applause was spotty and lukewarm. Plenty of people were losing money thanks to his ban.

The president smiled, thanked everyone for coming, and then lowered his voice to convey the gravity of what was to follow.

The huge screens behind him came to life.

"Members of Congress, our nation's business leaders, fellow Americans. Viruses are man's most treacherous enemy. They respect no borders, have no conscience, exhibit no mercy. They attack a mere cell at a time, yet they can reduce the human body to rubble in a matter of hours."

He paused for effect and stared sincerely into the cameras' big glass eyes.

Stunned by the graphic footage, those still murmuring fell silent.

"In their haste to reproduce," North continued, "viruses make mistakes. They replicate inaccurately. These near duplicates are not as harmless as we might hope. Rather, they become a new viral strain, capable of infecting others, perhaps even a different species from the host body they first occupied. Because of the speed with which they spread, the task of containing them is humbling."

The president paused again as the larger-than-life atrocities rolled on behind.

"Antibodies from the original host are ineffective in treating these new strains," the president said. "Today we face deadly varieties of hantavirus in every state in the Union. Swine flu kills thousands worldwide. Avian flu thousands more. AIDS marches on around the globe in a dozen deadly strains, many now heterosexual, all unstoppable. No one of us is safe. Even the air we breathe can become contaminated. As you know, the outbreaks in major American cities were a wake-up call. We took swift action. Still, we've lost hundreds of lives. Still, the virus spreads and evolves. The travel ban represents the only rational response to this new, shared reality. I am here today, in this special place…"

"To put on a show," someone shouted out.

North blinked, but ignored the heckler and continued, "…not only to seek Congressional understanding, but also to ask our business leaders for their continued patience and support. This afternoon, we received word that a new outbreak has occurred in Los Angeles. The CDC suspects that this may indeed be a new strain. In light of this, we have decided it is essential to place additional restraints on travel. Tonight I am expanding the ban to include all non-commercial rail and bus traffic.

Our Interstates will be open only to commercial truck-
ing and operators will be subject to health screenings at
checkpoints. Finally I am diverting all arriving cruises
ships at our ports of call."

The room went into an uproar.

North spread his arms like a preacher might.

The screen behind him went blood red. "This
plague has put us in grave jeopardy. We must constrain
the movement of people around this country!" North
pronounced.

The applause was fuller and more genuine this time.
Off stage, Barronson gave the word. "Now," he whispered into his headset.

Staffers soon rushed down the aisles carrying arm-
loads of paper.

"The reports we're handing out now document the
urgency of our situation," North said right on queue.

He gave the speaker several moments to calm the
room with his gavel.

"I will now take your questions," the president said.

North warmed up by choosing friends who threw
political soft balls enabling him to advance his agenda.
He cataloged how the ban on travel was already reliev-
ing pressure on the earth's endangered ecosystems,
cleaning the air, saving species. How families, re-united
at home, were reviving the idea of family itself—sharing, talking, lowering stress, even reversing the sale of
pharmaceuticals. He said something about increasing
disposable income that sounded particularly promising.

Then North acknowledged the Senator Duffy from

Nevada, a state that depended heavily on outside visitors. Forty million of them every year.

"Isn't it true, Mr. President," Duffy said, "that there are no reports of this virus outside our borders?"

"Every pandemic starts somewhere," North said politely, "then spreads unpredictably. Are you betting, Senator, that our future in this regard won't soon resemble our past?"

"I'm suggesting, Mr. President, that the nation's economy, indeed the world's, is already fragile. Encouraging a depression is a high price to pay to guard against an event that occurs rarely. Tourism is one of the most important—"

"I know," North interrupted him, "one in every seven workers." He squinted and his tone darkened. "Disease respects no political border," he lectured. "Every day the world's rainforests and rivers unleash new viruses—some will be more virulent, more unstoppable than the ones we face today. These parasites can be carried aboard a jet liner, or steamship, or as we have seen, aboard a private plane. Automobiles are hardly immune, Senator. Modern transportation is now quicker than viral incubation periods."

Duffy rose to protest, but the president ignored him. "No one knows in how many places these diseases hide between explosions. In rat fleas, mosquitoes, plant life, perhaps in soil itself. Brave men and women are putting their lives on the line to find out. They need time!"

The big screens came alive with grainy cell phone movies that captured the ugliness that ensued inside

Terminal B. Fist fights. Property damage. Trampled children. A surprising number of people turned out to be armed. Pipes' movie showed how civil authorities and regular folks had acted with empathy and concern, often at risk to themselves. There were heroes that day.

A hush fell over the auditorium for a second time. North's supporters, now more numerous than when the night began, started and sustained a low cheer, "Safe not sorry," that eventually filled the hall.

Barronson, confident North had turned the corner, decided it was time to deal with the president's most formidable enemies in Congress. He joined North for a moment at the podium, as if delivering a note. This was their signal to acknowledge the senior senator from Florida.

Franklin Broom was a rotund white-haired man, stereotypical of the country lawyers who had formed a solid southern voting block since Congress had opened its doors. He spoke for southern coastal states, which depended on tourism for solvency and were vehemently opposed to the ban. Broom's campaign coffers were stuffed with Disney money.

"Mr. President," Broom began in his ingratiating way, taking the opportunity to stand. "I speak for the voters, not only from the great state of Florida, but for citizens across this great land who have had their livelihoods undermined, their dreams dashed, their ability to plan their futures and manage their daily affairs put on hold by your proclamations. With all due respect sir, I must object—I am bound by the sacred duty that the Congress of the United States holds in regard to the financial well-being of the republic."

"Has the financial well-being of the republic been the senator's *highest* concern?" North blasted down at him.

"I welcome your examination of my record, Mr. President."

Chuckles emerged from every corner of the auditorium. Broom had been the subject of more than one ethics committee investigation. He looked around nervously.

"Mr. President," Broom said, pushing forward, "our investigation into this matter reveals that the federal government, that is to say, your administration, has quietly embarked on a very expensive program of—shall we call it—support."

"The federal government has put in place a safety net to justly compensate businesses most directly impacted by the ban," North said carefully. "What is the Senator suggesting?" he said, as if suddenly insulted.

"This support has the flavor of acquisition, Mr. President. With all due respect, an industry takeover."

"You, senator, should ask yourself what's the real bottom line here?" North said. "The safe keeping of the American people, or the next quarterly report of the corporations who guarantee your reelection?"

Broom cleared his throat as if to spit the president's words out. He persisted in a line of questioning that implied some conflict of interest lay behind the president's actions. "I can't help wondering if there might be some additional information that the White House might make available. Information that to date has, shall we say," Broom peered over his spectacles, "enjoyed only *limited* distribution?"

North gave him a big western smile. On the screen behind him a man from the Punon tribe in Borneo lay dying, a black, tar-like substance oozed from his nose and mouth.

"Perhaps the Senator has never seen a body ravaged by a retro-active disease," North said looking over his shoulder. "The headaches and nausea and fever give way to open sores and blood leaking from every orifice. The skin cracks open. The muscles in the face freeze into a mask of horror. Every organ—the stomach, liver, pancreas, even the brain—is attacked. You cough up your own insides, Senator. The sick do not fear death, they pray for it." North leaned into the bank of microphones. "I'm trying to save lives, Senator Broom. What are you willing to risk? The sons and daughters of Florida for the sake of one more ride at Disney World?"

The audience applauded enthusiastically as Senator Broom and his southern coalition, all on their feet in protest, were shouted down.

Pipes played his last card. The screens behind North now displayed the feed from a special web site where he was conducting a real-time vote on the president's actions. The tally was running four to one in favor of the president. So were the Tweets.

The house speaker called for a vote from those gathered inside the Center. "The people need to know where we stand," he said, asking for a show of hands.

His motion to extend and expand the travel ban "as long as public safety reasonably required it" was seconded by hundreds of raised hands, more than a few jumping on the North bandwagon for the first time when they saw the public opinion poll. Broom's southern gang bolstered by representatives from coastal states, plus Hawaii and Nevada, remained opposed. But twice their number, fearing any other position would be seen as reckless, backed the president. Non-voting business leaders signaled their approval with a steady applause.

North had carried the day.

"God bless," the president said. He put on his favorite white cowboy hat and stepped out of the spotlight.

There was confusion as the president left. Shoving others aside, Broom fought his way to the stage to say the vote was meaningless and non-binding. Then he accused North of bankrupting the tourism industry on purpose. But Barronson had turned the mics off and no one could hear him.

Lingering Congressional resistance was flattened by the tidal wave of support that poured into the White House over the next few days.

Pipes even floated a movement to curtail international travel. Several nations building new economies centered on tourism—Vietnam, Thailand, Cuba and Malaysia among them—held out, but many others promised to discuss travel restrictions of their own. India and China, terrified by what havoc a deadly virus might reek in their densely populated countries, and Algeria, where Islamic fundamentalists had been shooting tourists on-sight for years, supported North with limited travel bans of their own.

Pipes gave it all wings.

To the administration's great relief, Digital Darling temporarily faded from the headlines.

Chapter 27
No such agency

North, Darsk and Wilkins sat around the president's desk upstairs in the residency sharing pizza and beer. Between bites, North thumbed through the paperwork Darsk had handed him. It was a list of the world's best-known hackers and cyberpunks. Three hundred and seventy potential writers of the software already known around the nation's capital as "North's Bitch."

"Is she a bot or not?" the president asked, looking up at Darsk.

"With all due respect, sir, it doesn't make any difference. We don't believe she's self-generating, that is sentient. Someone is putting this show together, and that's real. Whether or not Digital Darling herself is real is not our current line of inquiry."

"Until someone has to run against her for a Senate seat," quipped Wilkins.

Darsk, an appointed official, ignored the jab.

"Let's toss out the Arabs and the Chinese," Darsk suggested, getting back to the business at hand. "That eliminates half the names."

"Who are we betting on?" Wilkins asked.

"Us," said Darsk.

"Not the Chinese?"

"No motive we can determine."

"Arabs?" Wilkins asked.

"No, they want planes in the air," Darsk said.

"I agree," said North. "This feels personal."

"Everyone on this list is a kid," the president said, scanning pages again. "Except this guy Brand—he's what, 78?"

"That's correct, sir," Darsk said. "We marginalized Brand some time back. He authored some of the original Internet code. Last of his crowd."

"Professor Bart Brand at M.I.T?" North asked. Brand had shredded his arguments in a debate years ago. North didn't take it well. He was all about winning. That's why Americans voted for him, after all.

"Same," Darsk said. "Somebody is taking a free ride on source code. To do that you need to know the net down to its nads. Brand qualifies."

"Where is he now? Wilkins asked.

"Southern Maine. I'll need to verify that." Darsk went on, "The list isn't complete, of course. These are the ones we can get to."

"Need more troops?" North asked.

"Thank you, Mr. President. "We just need more crunch time on the Crays, and I'm arranging that."

North looked over at Wilkins. "Send the Mexican up there?"

"Agent Poncho?" Darsk interrupted. "We've only had a few weeks with him, sir. Not really trained, actually."

Suddenly the small monitor on a nearby wall came to life. *The Digital Darling Show* came on.

"You see where she is today?" North said sharply. "In the damn Smithsonian. Right next door!"

Darsk looked to Wilkins and realized he wasn't going to get any help.

"Yes, Mr. President," he muttered, pulling out his cell phone.

Chapter 28
Perception management

According to the town records, Wide Waters comprised 125 acres, some 3,000 feet of which ran along the shore of Big Sebago Lake. The majestic main house, which now crowned the property, was surrounded on three sides by towering black pines and white birches. Beyond that lay fields of wildflowers, grazing pastures, wooded uplands and enough blueberry and blackberry bushes to support a good-sized village. At the water's edge, a log boathouse in the Adirondack style sheltered Bartholomew's collection of antique mahogany runabouts. Set back from that to one side was a barn, paddock and turnout for horses; on the other side there was a charming guest cottage.

Poncho squatted on the hood of his red Cadillac and took it all in through a pair of powerful binoculars. He could count sixteen Indian workers on the grounds. He thought he caught a glimpse of his target, Bartholomew Brand, in a second-floor window. He got up and got back into the convertible. He reached under the dash and hit a button. A false panel flipped down and presented two automatic Glock pistols. He rammed a 20-shot clip into one and tucked it into the shoulder holster he wore under his sport coat. He drove back down the gravel service road where he'd been parked, came around to the main drive, and drove right up to the front porch.

Cameras mounted in the tall pines signaled his approach. Joseph, who also served as Bartholomew's bodyguard, greeted Poncho on the front porch steps. One sniff and he knew Poncho, despite his foreign looks, was a cop of some kind.

Poncho eliminated any doubt by flashing his NSA badge.

Bartholomew had anticipated just such a visit. He was upstairs, in bed, an intravenous drip into the back of one hand. He practiced a consumptive cough.

Joseph let Poncho in, called upstairs on the house phone and signaled Poncho to follow him.

When they entered Bartholomew's bedroom, he smiled. With a slight quiver in his voice he invited Poncho to sit. "Please," he said gesturing toward a chair.

Instead, Poncho stood near the bottom of the bed and surveyed the room. The furnishings were mostly antique. There were two prescription bottles on the nightstand, and a dozen magazines scattered on the bed and floor. A wheelchair stood in one corner. He wondered if it had ever been used. There were no computers or television, just a radio.

"The last time I saw an NSA agent, the circumstances were much different," Bartholomew said.

"Wouldn't know about that," Poncho said.

"Of course," Bartholomew replied. He coughed for effect. "How can we help?"

Poncho said. "Checking in on how you been."

"As you see," Bartholomew answered.

Poncho looked around again. He picked up a framed photograph off the dresser. "Nice."

"My wife," Bartholomew said. "Deceased."

"Any children?"

"Sadly, no. My wife died rather young."

"Getting time for your bath," Joseph said.

"Yes. Joseph, please give the agent a tour of the house. Any room he'd care to visit. You're welcome to inspect the barn and outbuildings, as well."

Bartholomew coughed again, hoping he wasn't overdoing it.

Poncho gave him a toothy smile. "Start outside," he said.

Poncho wanted Bartholomew to be unnerved by the visit. He stared at him with wild eyes. He wanted Bartholomew to worry about who the hell was the government hiring these days.

What he didn't see as he left was Bartholomew hitting a small button under his nightstand to turn on a blinking red light in the barn's tack room.

Joseph escorted the Mexican downstairs then outside across the grounds and into the barn. Neither man spoke. Poncho took no interest in the animals. When they went out the far side doors, he swung the big Indian around and pushed him hard against the outside wall, the Glock pressed into his ribs.

"Now we talk," he said.

Joseph was unflustered. "Not today," he said, looking over Poncho's shoulder.

Poncho was used to having people cower when he pushed them around, and the Indian's cool demeanor surprised him. He sensed they were no longer alone. He released his grip on Joseph's shirt and turned slowly. A half dozen Passamaquoddy stood in a row, cradling shotguns and rifles.

"Perhaps we continue back inside the house," Poncho offered.

"Tour's over," said Joseph.

Chapter 29
Sustainability

By late July making war on the Feds was proving more monotonous than dangerous. The underground gang of three all suffered from the very cabin fever they were fighting to eradicate. Of the three, Carmen looked the most fatigued. Her easy smile had disappeared, replaced by something more intentional. She had lost interest in making everyone a salad every night. She was sleeping less. Seamus blamed himself and promised to open up the menu. He'd use the hibachi more, and to hell with Dave, they were going to eat in the roof garden after dark. Dave had bags under his eyes but Seamus guessed he was popping something better than Vitamin B and was prepared to keep on popping, taking Carmen along for the ride. As for himself, he needed to get out more, but he could always just do that. It was Carmen he was worried about.

Carmen and Dave both logged tedious hours in the studio where he wasn't always needed so he decided he'd go back to Faneuil Hall weekend afternoons. The show was fun, but not a paying job. He was out in the garage one morning tuning up the van's old engine when he hit upon an idea.

With a little help from Google, he located a nearby breeder and later that day returned to the brownstone with a magnificent pair of Afghan hounds.

Carmen was thrilled with the fancy dogs and named them Frankie & Johnny. "The Afghans," she said over Thai stir-fry, "will serve as proper introduction to people along the Promenade."

Even Dave, put off at first by the intrusion, had to admit that with their creamy coats and languorous strides the dogs were spellbinding.

One night Seamus thought he heard someone trying to break in downstairs. He woke the dogs, who were sleeping in the kitchen, and threw open the back door.

"Attack!" he commanded.

Instead of charging outside the dogs cowered under the kitchen table and started shaking and whimpering.

"What's going on?" Carmen asked, when he came back upstairs. "Did the dogs attack?"

Seamus shrugged his shoulders. "More like they had one," he said.

In the end, they all argued unattractively about who would feed them and train them and rub lanolin into their precious coats. Mostly Carmen complained bitterly about not being able to take them for a walk. For the first time since falling in love with her, Seamus wondered what the hell he was doing at 346 Beacon Street.

Chapter 30
Brand names in a non-existent world

W hen Poncho reported back to Darsk on his rendezvous with Bartholomew Brand, he left out a few details, particularly the one about him un-holstering his sidearm. Darsk eventually agreed that things sounded fishy, even for Maine.

"I'll scratch around MIT," he said to himself. Then to Poncho, "Stay up there until you hear from me."

MIT wasn't any help. Apropos of the leading-edge university, it didn't archive a hardcopy of anything that wasn't strictly required by either government, or large donors.

"We were the first university to go completely electronic," the provost told Darsk proudly.

Darsk had no trouble tracking Brand's career leading to his appointment to head up the New Media Lab, but testament to Bartholomew's exacting work just weeks before, there was no mention of a daughter. There were notations on the deaths of Bartholomew's wife and very recently, Uncle Bradford. Darsk's investigation also uncovered two cousins whom he quickly confirmed had been on safari in India for several months. That left a five-foot, 76-year old woman, widow of Bradford Perry, long-time resident of Damariscotta and life-long member of the Daughters of the American Revolution. A certain Letitia Perry, known to everyone, as the records properly noted, as Aunt Lottie.

Darsk instructed Poncho to head down east.

Poncho pulled into the picturesque village of Damariscotta the next morning.

The fishing village sat at the inland end of a deep ocean gorge. It was here that the river that gave its name to the town reached the sea. The village flanked both shores. Main Street featured the usual mix of quaint shops, weathered tourist attractions and historic homes, and a small bridge that connected two sides of town.

Poncho watched as the Lincoln County Rifle Club, the Second Congregational Church, Moon Shine Pottery and Waltz Rexall Drugs went past. Guns, religion and drugs, he thought, America the beautiful. He turned off the main street, drove two blocks down to the harbor and parked the Continental in front of Mariner Lumber Yard. He walked back up town and tried both Mexicali Blues and Two Fish, neither of which he discovered served food. Finally he settled on the Rising Tide Co-op Market where you could buy a sandwich.

"From away?" asked the middle-aged waitress.

Poncho had noticed the signs around town for the upcoming Founders' Day. "Yup," he said with a big smile. "Doing some work for the Founders' Day celebration."

"Big deal hereabouts," said the waitress. "What can

I getcha?"

"I'll try the tuna on toast," Poncho said.

"We don't get that tuna local, you know," the waitress counseled him with a friendly smile of her own. "Fried haddock's mighty good."

"Fried haddock," Poncho said. "And iced tea."

Poncho lingered over the sandwich. When the waitress returned he chatted her up.

"We're looking for some local folk to help with our part of the parade. Bringing in some antique cars," Poncho said. "You know, folks with roots to ride in the cars. Been looking for one Senora Lottie?"

"Aunt Lottie? Sure, she owns the lace shop across the street," the waitress said, pointing out the window. "Got yourself a live one there."

Poncho left a big tip.

The shop across the street said Arsenic and Old Lace. Wonder why, he thought, opening the door.

The conversation with Lottie started rough. She was immediately suspicious when he used Bartholomew as a reference, and he could tell she didn't like his looks. The conversation went nowhere. Her answers didn't even make sense to Poncho. The encounter then ended badly. Lottie explaining in no uncertain terms she didn't own a computer or cared to, didn't watch much TV and knew nothing of this so-called Digital Darling.

"Isn't anybody around here," she said convincingly. "Want to know something about the Brands ask that crooked banker in Boston, something-or-other Holliston. Now scoot."

Poncho wanted to threaten her, shoot her maybe, but she was the only lead he had. He walked back to the car, looked around for a place to take a piss and noticed a Men's sign on the side of the lumberyard building. He filled the urinal then turned around to use the sink. Hanging on the back of the door was the old yellowed cover of a Mexican magazine he'd read as a kid. On it, a beautiful young girl posed before the ancient ruins in his homeland. The closer Poncho looked, the more that young girl looked like Digital Darling.

"Everybody's lying," Poncho hissed.

He tore the magazine cover from the wall and headed back to Arsenic and Old Lace. The shop was open, but empty. He called out but got no response. Impatient, he went behind the counter and through the curtained doorway leading out back. In the rear of the shop Lottie's body lay on the floor. Her face wore a look of disbelief interrupted by pain. Bruises had already formed on her neck.

Chapter 31
Dysfunctional
family feud

The brownstone wasn't air-conditioned and the August heat in Boston broke records. It took a weighty toll on the show's creators.

Seamus sat by helplessly as Carmen became more distant and unfocused, even when they made love. She was there, but somewhere else, too. Real enough to light up a billion screens only to disappear into the ether Bartholomew had given her to breathe. The public life she'd dreamed of in Boston hadn't panned out, either. She was becoming a star, but not a flesh and blood one. Seamus feared the sweet and sassy woman he'd met not so long ago was becoming two unhappy women. The first was invisible, the second was untouchable.

Carmen didn't talk much about her father and Seamus wondered how deep her loyalty toward him and revenge toward the government ran. Suppose their situation went from hunkering down to outright siege? And what would *he* do if things got sticky?

One morning he and Dave were up early in the kitchen. Dave sat at the breakfast table over iced coffee.

Seamus poured himself a glass and took a casual inventory of the refrigerator. Leftover pizza and pad thai, Dave's shelf of supplements and his stash of pepperoni sticks. Nothing for dinner.

"I don't see why Carmen couldn't wear a wig or big hat and get some sun in the garden," Seamus said.

"That's why you run errands," Dave said without interest.

"How long are we going to do this?" Seamus asked.

"Until someone in the White House laughs at *Will & Grace*," Dave said.

"Carmen isn't eating," Seamus said. "She's not sleeping well either. I'm not standing by while she's reduced to pixel dust."

Dave looked up at him and cooed. "John iPad Wayne, look at you."

Seamus wanted to get at the heart of what drove Dave and changed the subject. "Not everyone who works for the government is an asshole," he said.

"How would you know? And how would you know if you were an asshole? Speaking of which, aren't you a little past your sell-by date around here?"

"I'm in love with her."

"Ha!" Dave said. "Can you see the front of the line from where you are, cowboy?"

"So you keep her alive like some zoo animal?" Seamus said angrily. "Because she's got a goddam audience?"

"She's an idea," Dave said, pouring more milk into his coffee. "Ideas aren't owned anymore. They emerge, dissolve and reassemble."

"Digital bullshit," Seamus said. "How about some reruns? Give her some digital time off."

"All we have is the head start Bartholomew gave us. One generation of software. A few months."

"Why does she have to be sacrificed?"

"Because goddam sissified patriotism doesn't get it done."

"So sacrifice yourself."

"Nobody wants to hear it from a fag!"

"Girls, girls," Carmen said as she breezed into the room. "It's hot. We're all tired. Bad enough I'm all cooped up without you two squabbling. Listen, I've got an idea. It's Saturday. The streets will be packed with my look-alikes tonight. I'll wear a disguise. It'll be safe. Let's go to Café 29 for dinner and sit outside."

"Great idea," Seamus said. "There's nothing in the frig to eat anyway. I'll make a reservation."

"Davie, please." Carmen wrapped her arms around him. "Everyone will be there."

He finally relented. "Well, 29 *is* my favorite S&M family restaurant."

"Describes us perfectly," Carmen said.

Chapter 32
Like it never
even happened

Back at the makeshift NSA office in Boston, Poncho waited patiently as the printer spit out the information he needed about James Holliston. Poncho called Darsk in Maryland and was instructed to pay the banker a visit in Wellesley. Chat a while.

Early the next morning, Poncho drove through a series of fashionable suburbs to an address in Wellesley and when he saw the morning papers laying in Holliston's drive, parked the red Continental nearby. He hadn't waited twenty minutes when the banker walked down in his bathrobe to retrieve them.

Poncho was out of the car, holding up a copy of the magazine cover picturing Carmen as he approached the banker.

"You tell me where," Poncho said coming up to him.

Holliston looked at the Mexican with disdain and tried to turn away. Poncho blocked his path and flashed a badge.

The banker considered the brown-skin man holding it, and dismissed the badge as a forgery. "I don't know who you are," he said, "but this conversation is not going to take place."

"We talk or bad things happen."

Poncho said it so nonchalantly Holliston could feel his bowels move.

"If you are who you say you are, talk to my lawyer," Holliston said.

"Talkin' to you," Poncho said.

"Listen mister, this isn't how we do business in Boston. Screw with me and every badge in New England will be looking for *you*."

Just then a neighbor drove up, stopped, looked quizzically at Poncho, and asked Holliston if he was going to watch their kids play Little League that night. Holliston waved, said he'd be there, then used the occasion to get away from his interrogator.

"Always with the leaving," Poncho said in frustration as Holliston rushed back up the drive.

A half hour later, the banker got into his Mercedes Silver Edition coupe, and as he drove down the driveway tripped the two charges Poncho had planted near the granite towers that flanked the home's impressive entrance. James T. Holliston, faithful husband, father of two, esteemed member of a dozen non-profit boards, along with his luxury sedan was blown high into the dewy suburban air and across the well-manicured yards of his slumbering neighbors.

Riding back to town, Poncho almost didn't hear the explosion. *Rigoletto* was blasting from the car's CD player. Through the door of his hotel room an hour later, he could hear a phone ringing.

"Nothing has exploded in Wellesley since the Revolutionary War!" Darsk screamed into his ear the minute he picked up the phone on his nightstand.

Poncho shrugged his shoulders as if the situation required no special explanation.

"What the fuck," he said to Darsk.

"Whaaaat? I'll tell you what the fuckin' whaat. A witness put you at the scene. That's fuckin' what! Just like up in Maine."

"Didn't kill da loco chica," Poncho said without emotion.

"Everywhere you go, someone dies."

"Yeah," Poncho said. "Been like that."

"We could have talked sensibly to him. Explained our mission, maybe. Appealed to his love of country."

Guy showed no respect, Poncho was thinking.

"I can't fuckin' believe it," Darsk's voice boomed. "Why didn't you just go into the house and blow away the whole family?"

Poncho twisted the phone until its plastic casing cracked. He threw it against the wall. He sat down heavily on the bed. Darsk was still screaming through the broken earpiece.

"Tell me you found out where she is," Darsk implored. "Tell me this isn't another fuckin' dead end."

Poncho didn't answer. His boss was working up to something. Let the clown go.

"You're history on this." Darsk said. Then finally, in a calm tone, "Starting now. You hear me?"

Poncho stomped on the parts until the sound stopped.

It was 11:25 AM when he left his room. He kept his lunch date at a local restaurant with a gorgeous Japanese in-line skating queen he'd hooked up with on the Internet. They split the salmon special. Before they'd finished the chardonnay, Poncho was back on the case. That's when Director Darsk conveyed the news of one, maybe two, unfortunate deaths to the chief of staff.

"Sounds like he's the only one making progress," Wilkins said sarcastically. "Put him in charge."

Chapter 33
Afghanistan

C armen had come a long way from the shores of Big Sebago to become the center of national attention, and becoming Digital Darling was worth the ride. No matter how it ended, she would be remembered. Mass media was magical in Dave's hands, plus her on-screen role was a constant reminder of a fairytale youth. So was rummaging through the big steamer trunk, merrily trying on an assortment of slinky and sequined little black dresses, silk suits from Paris and slippery undergarments. Ever since she'd arrived in town, Boston had laid at her feet, tantalizingly close but out of reach. Tonight, her sacrifice and hard work would be rewarded.

At last she paraded before Seamus in a casual, creamy summer knit and strappy sandals that both accented her height and clung to her proportioned curves. He gave her a big thumbs up.

At the front door, Dave insisted she wear a hat to hide her signature hair.

Not wanting to disturb the peace, she ran back

upstairs and returned sporting an oversized black silk beret under which she'd manage to cover all of it.

"It's trans-occasional," Dave agreed, still uneasy about the evening out.

Reservations at Café 29 in hand and the twin Afghans in tow, they set out for the Promenade. They were all feeling giddy.

For Carmen's enjoyment, Seamus suggested they take the long way, walking first down Beacon Street and through the Public Garden, strolling arm-in-arm under the trees arched over the serpentine pathways, between the well-manicured flower beds, past the swan boats and the long shadow cast by the statue of General George Washington astride his horse. The Afghans pulled at their leashes, eager to engage the squirrels that were busy gathering acorns in anticipation of cooler nights. Like everyone else, the squirrels sensed the dogs were no threat.

"Suppose someone asks me if I'm the real Digital Darling?" Carmen said.

"Say yes," Seamus said. "No one will believe you."

"I agree," said Dave.

On Newbury Street, the trio got a first-hand look at how popular their underground travel show had become: Digital Darling paraphernalia was center stage in every other store window. In the office windows above the storefronts, plastic surgeons and dermatologists advertised look-alike adjustments. As they walked along they passed by dozens of Digital Darling poseurs, one of whom, with obvious envy, stopped to compliment

Carmen, "You look *so much* like her," the girl gushed.

"You've never seen her without make-up," Dave said, dismissing the admirer. The comment made him nervous all over again. When Carmen wanted to go into one shop to complain that the commemorative dinnerware on sale didn't look anything like the real Digital Darling, Dave pulled up outside and scolded both of them. "Get it right. We're not here."

At the Café, they got a front row sidewalk table and relaxed with a round of drinks and enthusiastic talk about the menu. Dave knew the maitre d'—a slight green-eyed boy with whom he'd had a brief but volcanic affair.

"I'm having artic char and arugula and lots of wine," Carmen announced. "And a fancy dessert. And cognac!"

Seamus was glad to see her appetite return. Even though he'd made an effort to grill more food outside, Carmen was living largely on saltines and puffed wheat.

The dogs sat on either side of her like temple lions. Whenever she spoke they looked up in adoring anticipation.

⸺⸻⸻◆⸻⸺

At the other end of the Promenade in the dingy 3rd floor offices rented by the NSA, Poncho organized a contingent of six agents, most of whom were grumbling about having to work on a Saturday night. Once again, Poncho had gotten his way to try something Darsk considered too risky. With the new government emphasis on gathering info at the street level, North and Wilkins gave the go-ahead over the director's objections.

Poncho slapped his hand against the street map that highlighted the location of every restaurant and outdoor cafe along Newbury Street. He was wearing a black eye patch and starched white shirt. He looked like the Mexican Hathaway Man.

"The three of us," he said, pointing at two agents, "go down this side of the street. You three follow on the other side. Pace yourself. And check the parked cars. No badges, weapons concealed. Respectful—leave the cash on the tables and load the look-alike chicas into the vans, nice and easy."

Poncho clicked his headset on. "Channel 19 is hot. Questions?"

One after another the agents acknowledged network reception.

"Suppose somebody won't go?" an agent asked.

"No grabbing asses. If the boyfriend wants to come along, OK—we sort that out later."

Everyone groaned. More paperwork.

"By the numbers." Poncho said it firmly. If successful, the NSA would conduct roundups all over the country. Fuck Darsk.

"Mount up," Poncho said.

The agents left in teams. The festive crowds that gave Boston's international dating scene its allure easily absorbed them.

⟫●⟪

Carmen, Seamus and Dave sat eight blocks away Carmen had just washed down the arugula, blue cheese and walnut salad with her second glass of wine. Dave was on his third Absolute and tonic. Even Seamus had had two beers.

For the first time since growing up in Philadelphia, Seamus appreciated the palpable city energy. Where Sturbridge said relax, Boston said get excited. Where the country's heart beat to the rhythm of nature, the city was fueled by senses piqued by pharmaceuticals and chance encounters. He slowly ate his fillet and corn salsa and listened while Dave and Carmen swapped snide remarks about the most tasteless look-alike outfits parading up and down the sidewalk.

Up the street, the roundup was going more smoothly than expected. Not because of competence or tact on the part of the NSA agents, but because of the surprising willingness of Digital Darling impersonators to hop into the vans. Some simply desired attention, or hoped for a YouTube hit, or a local talk show appearance. A sincere few were trying to make a political point. All were there to build an audience.

Following the script, Poncho pretended to be a representative of Vibe Media. He handed out a special number and when recipients texted back, they earned free drinks at the establishment. Then look-alikes were asked if they'd like to tell their story on camera.

Government vans were conveniently parked at every cross street. Within an hour the NSA had corralled 32 suspects, half of whom, though aided considerably by make-up, wigs and miscellaneous DDware, didn't really look much like Digital Darling.

"Book 'em all," said Poncho over Channel 19, "If they *think* they're Digital Darling, maybe the fuck they are."

Back down the street at Café 29, Carmen was explaining her look-alike status as entirely coincidental. Other patrons were sharing the latest travel news with her, keeping the buzz alive. A drug cartel, one diner claimed, secretly owned American Airlines and The Princess Cruise Lines and maybe Kakas Shipping, too.

"Have you read the blogs about North's attack on Disney? The president called them unpatriotic. Some say Disney is the real patriot. And North is up to something."

Carmen feigned indifference and was careful not to know too much.

"I don't like to travel," she said innocently.

"We're attracting too much attention," Seamus muttered.

———⇒●⇐———

A man ran up to the maitre d' and pointed back up the street. Seamus noticed, but couldn't hear what was said.

Dave was absorbed in a conversation about the merits of extreme reality programming with an attractive man at the next table. Then he suddenly turned back toward Carmen and Seamus. "Listen," he said.

Carmen and Seamus could hear it, too. The Saturday night noise drifting down the Promenade had grown discordant, punctuated with shouts, peeling tires, and the excited screams of patrons. People in the restaurant began un-pocketing their cell phones anticipating a photo op.

Dave waived the maitre d' over to their table.

"Some sort of raid," he told them. Then, nodding in Carmen's direction, "They're gonna want her for sure."

The trio was on their feet in an instant. As Carmen got up, the woman sitting in the chair behind her grabbed her beret. Carmen's trademark golden hair tumbled down around her shoulders. For one of the few times in her life she was scared.

Everyone applauded and whistled loudly.

"It's *her*," a woman shouted.

Carmen desperately stuffed her hair back under the beret.

"Naw," said the man sitting next to her. "You can't tell."

But the episode had created an uproar.

Seamus elbowed Dave, "I'll take the dogs and go through the park. Get her out of here."

Poncho was less than a block away when he heard the cheers and whistles rise from Café 29. He jumped up on a nearby table to get a better view. Even at this distance he caught a glimpse of Carmen—the hair, the glow—there was something special about this look-alike. His plan *was* going to pay off. He could see she wasn't alone. There was another woman, no, a man with a red-haired pony tail, moving through the tables with her. They disappeared inside. At the same time, a man leading two large dogs left and headed the other way.

"Everyone into the alley behind Café 29," Poncho yelled into his mouth mic. "I'll go in the front. Pronto goddamit!"

He barked the orders as he ran. When he reached the Café, the maitre d' blocked the door.

"What was the name on that reservation?" the maitre d' asked casually.

Poncho tossed him aside.

The restaurant was packed and his prey was nowhere in sight. Poncho pushed his way into both restrooms despite objections and finding nothing headed for the kitchen door. A huge man in a bloodstained apron and brandishing a cleaver blocked his way. There was no other passage to the alley except circling the entire block, so Poncho decided he'd better catch up with the dog man.

"I'll be back for your pasty ass," he threatened the maitre d' on the way out.

The pretty boy looked up and grinned. "Need a reservation for that, too."

At the end of the Promenade, Seamus had crossed into the Public Garden and was headed for the Boston Common to lead authorities away from Carmen and Dave.

In a full sprint, Poncho made up the distance by the time Seamus and the Afghans neared an exit on the far side. He spun Seamus around.

"Not who you're looking for," Seamus said, meeting his dark eyes.

"I decide."

"Take your time," Seamus said.

A voice came over Poncho's earpiece. "We missed them in the alley. Got some problems up here, boss, better get back."

Poncho spit on Seamus' shoes. "Some day you see me again," he warned.

For the first time in their lives, the Afghans growled.

Poncho squatted down as if to admire the spectacular dogs. He scratched their ears and brought their heads together. In the darkness he pulled out a knife, and before Seamus could stop him he slit Frankie's & Johnny's throats.

Chapter 34
Mad men

I nside the NSA it's called Signal Intelligence. Banks of super computers continuously scan the world's communications networks for key words and phrases. "All relevant documents" are assembled. Thousands of eagle-eyed employees then sort through the transmissions, searching for information and misinformation. There are markets for both.

Despite the dedication of Darsk's Digital Darling hit team, three months had produced no solid leads. In the absence of anything else, Poncho's deadly rampage and disruptive roundups were seen as progress, and that put Darsk in a particularly foul mood.

"Problems?" he yelled at anyone who would listen. "What makes you think we got problems? We got dope dealers on marine radios in south Florida telling us to stick the travel ban up our ass. Last night, some gun-happy border guard in Arizona mistakenly shot five Americans crossing into Mexico. *Into* Mexico!"

Darsk also dreaded an inevitable call from the FBI demanding to know why his operatives were executing

Boston bankers with Mayflower last names. At this point he was sure of only two things: he was sick of being over-ruled by the White House, and if he ever got his hands on that blonde bitch, he was personally going to strangle her. He also fantasized about neutralizing Poncho.

———————————

Pipes Barronson, meanwhile, was faring better. He had opened a new front on the war by bringing in Constitutional scholars to refute the argument that First Amendment rights should extend to individuals clearly intent on disrupting the peace. You owed your country allegiance even during questionable times, they argued. He handed out talking points on why citizenship isn't free to spokespersons from the State Department, Interior, Commerce and Education. The Pentagon, Office of Budget & Management, even the Library of Congress added their spin to the crafted narrative. The definition of patriotism was twisted and tweaked more than at any time since Thomas Paine.

Pipes also flooded the media with invectives that linked Digital Darling to everyone from Lizzie Borden to Osama bin Laden. Whenever possible he quoted CDC statistics tracking every incident of communicable dis-ease on the move and suggesting it was America-bound. Likewise, he squelched any dialog that the Born-1 virus had burnt itself out.

His media machine released inspiring stories about drug enforcement agents, members of the Coast Guard and Marines, border guards, agency liaison people, citizen watchdogs, half the medical establishment. All were congratulated by an appreciative administration for protecting the public welfare while rightly questioning the sincerity and patriotism of those who supported the Digital Darling movement.

Despite the monumental effort and near complete compliance by the mainstream press, as Labor Day approached *The Digital Darling Show* was knocking out a solid 35 share and look-alikes were estimated in the tens of thousands nationwide.

Darsk sat at his desk in a funk, staring at the magazine cover Poncho had brought back from Damariscotta. The paper was brown and the coating had worn off the cover stock. Was it her? A fair resemblance, but there was no way to be sure. The world was filled with good-looking blondes. The magazine had long since gone out of business and no one had been able to locate the archives. He painted the page with a special glaze and held the stained and tattered cover up to the light. Near the bottom, on the reverse side, the faint outline of some broken type was just noticeable. He dampened the paper with a contrast gel, and increased the light source. He got out a Spanish dictionary. He scribbled down dozens of possibilities and reworked what the letters might spell. Even with the help of deciphering software, it took him over an hour:

Crédito de la foto: Casaba Rendor

"The photographer," he said, turning back to his computer.

He keyed in a Search and Identity Request. Four billion personnel files were scanned. Casaba's biography came back in eighteen seconds.

The data was sketchy. It included childhood references to his family in Hungary.

His circus name, *The Incredible Casaba*, appeared on an old handbill. He was a juggler. Also incredible, he had once worked for the CIA taking photographs of U.S. politicians and world leaders in so-called "situations." Darsk knew that meant in the company of prostitutes or strippers, more than occasionally, young men. The Agency kept the intelligence on file, just in case. Casaba had a home address.

"I'll be dammed," Darsk said, printing out the data.

He was yelling again, storming out of his office, waving Casaba's profile in the air. "I want this guy picked up yesterday. A team on this doorstep, now. Move! Somebody better put a report on my desk by the time I take a piss!"

Eight or nine people fled the room.

———————

Two NSA operatives in trench coats and sunglasses stayed downstairs. Two others climbed the narrow wooden stairs to the fifth floor of a row house in the mostly Black southeast section of Washington D.C. They knocked loudly on Casaba Rendor's door. When he didn't answer, they kicked it in.

The one-room apartment was a pit. The bed was piled four-feet high with blankets and dirty clothes. A rusty RV kitchen unit stood next to an open-pipe sink in one corner. An old chrome-legged table with a floral laminated top and two chairs with torn Naugahyde seat covers sat in the opposite corner. A bedspread had been draped over the only window. Several small pieces of old oak furniture covered with dead varnish and dust were spaced around the room. The place was dank and smelled of foreign tobaccos. In the 60-watt light the agents could make out large photographs of women, most in various stages of undress, covering the walls.

Nothing moved. They put away their guns and began searching.

One checked out the bathroom. It was littered with over-the-counter creams and plastic kitchen utensils. Props, the agent wondered, for some elaborate form of masturbation? On the back of the door hung several pictures of a beautiful young girl posing before Mayan temples. The agent tore the photos off the wall.

"This is the place," he called out to his partner.

His partner was rummaging through the dresser. Finding nothing of interest, he kicked the pile on the unmade bed and thought he heard a groan. He kicked even harder to remove any doubt. Yanking off several layers, he found a terrified little man with twisted features curled up in a ball.

"Call it in," the agent said. "We have a winner."

Chapter 35
An isolated incident

A few days earlier, when Joseph had returned from Damariscotta, he gave Bartholomew a knowing look. Bartholomew was furious that he hadn't anticipated a problem with Lottie, and mad at himself for ending up on the NSA list. He reasoned the agency—in the form of that scary Mexican—would be back. He and Joseph began preparing for an old fashioned war.

—————>●<—————

On Labor Day, a perfect late summer day in the lakes region of southern Maine, Poncho stood re-adjusting his 30-power binoculars. He was up in the plastic observation bubble of a Winnebago requisitioned from the Agency's Visual Information Branch. The RV was parked on a dirt road at the northwest edge of the Brand property. The road had been blocked off at either end. Local cops had been told to attend to business elsewhere. From his perch, Poncho would command the planned offensive. The main cluster of buildings at Wide Waters came into focus. A small digital printout at the edge of his eyepiece blinked "1200 Yd."

He would do it big and splashy, just like Hollywood. When the NSA had refused to authorize helicopters, Poncho arranged for his old friends at Warriors to provide two birds.

The two fully armed BlackHawks now approached the estate flying low, just feet above the water. They sped eastward, hidden by the sun to their rear, their engines muffled by a steady northeast headwind. They came out of nowhere.

For two centuries Wide Waters manor had stood like a proud eagle, commanding the landscape, surveying the vast watery domain, ever alert to danger. It had withstood rapacious developers, Mother Nature in high pitch, intrusive utilities, even the famous Whiskey Wars of the 1930s. It was an implacable monument.

"It's a sitting duck," Poncho said into the radio net.

The Blackhawks closed in. They circled above the main house for several minutes, a loudspeaker voice demanding that everyone inside come out with their hands in the air.

As Poncho hoped, no one surrendered.

The stablehand Bartholomew had placed on guard duty up in the widow's walk was terrified. Both helicopters had made one pass directly over his head and scared the living bejesus out of him. Then they split up. One spun in mid-air just a hundred yards beyond the house. The second hovered ominously at the water's edge, guns trained on the house.

"Primo objecto," Poncho directed from the RV, "Brand alive and the house intact. Collateral damage, no problemo."

Poncho looked around at his gung-ho lieutenants in the Winnebago. "Anyone off plan," he said into his headset, "wakes up with his balls in his mouth."

He flashed a wet toothy smile. "Green light," Poncho ordered.

The helicopters unloaded dozens of smoke and gas canisters in the direction of the exquisite lead-glass windows of the manor house. The pilots watched in amazement as the munitions bounced back, exploding harmlessly in the yard. Bartholomew had covered the priceless windows with jet-age plastic years ago for protection against the bone-chilling winter wind, a stray hunter's bullet, and perhaps—in the back of his mind— an evening just like this. From more than a few feet away, the plastic was invisible.

The chopper pilots wasted more rounds, eventually their full consignment on the smaller windows upstairs, similarly protected, and succeeded only in unleashing so much smoke their target disappeared entirely.

Bartholomew was now up on the widow's walk, blasting away with a shotgun at the choppers. When one pilot's request for permission to use incendiary rockets was denied by Poncho, both choppers backed off a few hundred yards and stayed airborne above the vast berry fields.

Standing next to Bartholomew on the roof, camera in hand, Joseph got it all on film.

Back in the Winnebago, Poncho was watching the

live feed from the choppers' nose-mounted minicams until smoke turned the monitors gray.

"Jesus Christo!" he yelled three times into his headset.

"Place is tighter than a virgin's ass, sir," said the pilot in chopper one. "We've got plenty to pump in there, though, just give us the word."

Before Poncho could answer, the radio operator to his right said, "We've got curious state troopers on the main road, Sir."

"Start a fire in the woods. And close off that fuckin' road."

"The choppers?"

"Set'em down."

"Ramirez, line three, you ready?" Poncho barked. "We're going in on foot. What? They're just fucking Indians! Mount up!"

With the helicopters at bay, Bartholomew rushed downstairs to the main hall of the house and handed out automatic rifles and ammo from hidden wall cases to his small Passamaquoddy army. He reminded them of their roles, to watch out for each other, to remain calm when the chaos of gunfire began. Counting Joseph and himself, they numbered 27.

Bartholomew jammed fresh shells into a pump-action 16-gauge as he talked. "I promise the world will remember the stand you took here," he said to his troops. "Remember, lead the action toward the cameras on the front of the house."

Joseph encouraged them. "Take up your positions... wait for my signal."

The guard from the roof ran into the hallway. "They're coming," he said.

Bartholomew strapped twin Colt pistols that belonged to his great grandfather around his waist. "Put this in your belt, and keep the camera running," he said, handing Joseph a small pearl-handled derringer. The derringer was a gift to his wife from the Washburn side of the family—from an uncle who had founded the Pinkerton Guards. Bartholomew appreciated the irony.

———————

Since Poncho couldn't be sure of the exact number of enemy Indians, he had commissioned two armored jeeps filled with US Army troops, to back up the NSA agents.

The NSA men now made their way down from the dirt road into the berry fields. After a hundred yards they were all bleeding badly in the high thorny bushes. The Indians could hear them cursing and started shooting. Unable to see their enemy, the NSA foot soldiers lobbed mortars. One landed on the barn roof and set the hayloft afire.

Several stablehands ran madly through the smoke-filled barn opening up the stalls, and forcing the horses out. Peppermint and Dobson, his playmate since Carmen had arranged her shipment from the farm near Sturbridge Village, galloped into the large paddock at the rear of the barn. Peppermint circled inside the high-railed fence twice. He picked up speed on the second lap and made a determined leap. He cleared the fence with the front of his powerful body; his rear hooves knocked off the top railing. He stopped and spun round on the far side and reared up as if to show the mare how much bigger horses were than fences. This, the gunfire, and the missing top rail gave Dobson the nerve to try. She followed in his path and with a mighty urge cleared the fence herself. The horses galloped shoulder-to-shoulder up the back driveway, through the meadows and finally disappeared into the far woods where Carmen had so often guided Peppermint.

Back up on the widow's walk, Joseph got their escape on camera.

The barn, the livery stable and the one end of the main house were now in flames. In the paddock, several Passamaquoddy were hitching the nervous horses held behind to carriages. When the NSA troops finally broke out of the berry fields, they rushed into the middle of the huge circular drive, finding little cover. Joseph gave the signal—an incredible war hoop—and the Indians encircled the NSA forces guns blazing from the carriages. Others firing from the guesthouse helped cut the hapless Feds to ribbons in a crossfire.

The victory was sweet, but short-lived. The armored jeeps, slowed briefly by mud and stone walls, finally arrived with machine guns rattling. They slaughtered the horses and drove the surviving Passamaquoddy down toward the lake where they took what shelter they could among the shoreline rocks.

———>●<———

Inside the manor house, Bartholomew realized there wasn't much time. He and Joseph ran to his office, government agents not far behind. They managed to shut the hidden door to the lab behind them just in time.

"Give me the camera," Bartholomew said. He set it on a high shelf and plugged it into the computer that was recording the feed from all the other cameras. He dialed the secret access number to the studio in Boston.

Just outside the lab door, troops were smashing through the bookshelves. Bartholomew pumped two shots at the entry way and directed Joseph to stand in the far corner of the lab next to the main console.

"Wait as long as you dare," he said to him, "then hit the SEND button.

An instant later, NSA troops blew the lab door off with plastic explosives and four agents, followed by Poncho, burst into the room.

This was the second time the government had violated his laboratory, and Bartholomew determined it would be the last.

"Forgive me, darling," he said looking up at the camera, then spun around and unloaded his shotgun.

A deafening barrage of return fire ensued.

In the far corner of the room Joseph got up off the floor slowly with one hand raised, the derringer dangling from his thumb in surrender. The agents hesitated for just a second.

When they did, Joseph hit the button.

Chapter 36
Connecting the dots

Seamus spent Labor Day at Faneuil Hall. He welcomed the time out of the brownstone, which had taken on the feeling of a bunker. Worse, he wasn't sure if this planned time away was a prelude to his own end game. He longed for his predictable life back in the Village, and worried he couldn't build anything real with Carmen outside her fleeting digital world.

Only a handful of tourists who had managed to skirt the travel ban and a few Bostonians who hadn't evacuated to the Cape, islands, or northern lakes wandered by, most looking like they wished they were somewhere else. He sold two pots.

Seamus was re-filling the van's display racks when he heard a familiar voice.

"Long time, Agent McGuire," Darsk said.

Seamus spun around unable to hide his dismay.

"How's the pottery thing going?"

"Got one good client."

"Everybody finds their way," Darsk said, as if talking about himself. Then, pointing to the pots, "Like the ones with the antelopes on them."

"Some of my favorites," Seamus said.

Darsk gave Seamus the kind of thin-lipped smile a perturbed father might give an errant son just before smacking him around. "The shit chat is over," he said.

Seamus felt control over his life slipping away. "What's the job?" he said.

"We believe Digital Darling, whoever, is in Boston," Darsk said. "We might need a shooter."

"Might do more good just keeping an eye out from here," Seamus said, thinking that's exactly how he'd met Carmen.

"Like you to meet the team," Darsk said. "Now, actually."

Seamus reversed what he was doing and began unloading the display racks and repacking the pots. He collected his thoughts. If Darsk was meeting him at the van that meant the studio was still a secret. Still, they had narrowed their search to Boston.

"Somebody up there must like you," Darsk said finally, shaking his head.

"How's that?" Seamus said.

"Chance to redeem yourself in the agency's eyes."

Seamus had wondered if this day would ever come. It'd been ten years. Word had filtered down from time to time: He was part of an experimental program, deep cover agents disguised as artists. Artists mix with important people, so the strategy went. At least his limbo status with the agency was over. But this was going to be tricky. If they wanted him back now, that meant every resource was being called up. It meant the agency was either so close they could smell their prey, or they were willing to make a lot of noise even if they were wrong. He could no longer risk going anywhere near the brownstone.

"Give me your cell phone," Darsk said back in his car, as if anticipating Seamus' next move.

———————

Back in the brownstone studio, Carmen and Dave were thunderstruck by the horrific broadcast from Maine.

Carmen sat incapacitated, watching her home destroyed and her father gunned down like a criminal. "This can't be real. Is it real, Davie? My god, Daddy!"

Before Dave could console her, Carmen started throwing things—pillows, light stands, even one of Seamus' pots. She screeched out her father's name so loudly, Dave temporarily lost his hearing.

Unable to calm her down, Dave managed to pour fruit juice laced with Seconal down her throat, and when she collapsed in his arms he carried her into her bedroom.

He tried to gauge how long it would take before the government pinpointed their location. They'd pick through everything at the lab in Maine, but that would take weeks. They wouldn't hesitate to torture the Passamaquoddy, but if he knew Bartholomew, even Joseph would know nothing. So how long did they have? Without Bartholomew to throw inquisitors off track, it wouldn't be enough. He spent the rest of the day activating the software that would shut down the broadcast automatically, and then destroy the studio's data banks. He gathered up all the paperwork and written notes he could find and piled them on the hearth downstairs for a bonfire. He contacted friends operating a sub-rosa travel service and reserved the last two seats on the next chartered plane leaving Hanscom Field for points south, preferably Key West.

Two seats. Could he get Carmen on that plane without Seamus?

———————

From a coffee shop across the street, Poncho saw the guy with the two afghans and Director Darsk enter the building where the NSA kept offices. He couldn't believe his eyes. He waited a few minutes then followed them into the small lobby.

The elevator had left and stopped on the third floor. Poncho took the stairs. Just as Seamus entered the NSA office behind Darsk, Poncho rushed him. They tumbled onto the office floor, knocking over furniture. Poncho ended up straddling Seamus and pushed a Glock up under the potter's cheekbone.

"Dead man," he said.

"Put it away," Darsk commanded.

"He's hiding her."

"You're a rookie," Seamus said calmly.

"Show you what kinda rookie," the Mexican said.

"Back off," Darsk yelled. "He works for us."

Poncho pulled the magazine cover picturing Carmen off Darsk's desk and shoved it in Seamus' face.

"Look familiar?" he said, re-holstering his gun.

"I watch television," Seamus said.

"Picture not on television." Poncho turned to Darsk. "He was with her the night of the sweep. Swear on the Madre Virgen."

"Why didn't you arrest him then?" Darsk said.

"Why didn't I kill him," Poncho said, slowly letting Seamus up.

Seamus dusted himself off. "Cuts in the training budget?" he asked Darsk.

"Agent Poncho is on special assignment from Executive. Now sit, both of you."

"I kill you for fun," Poncho whispered to Seamus as they both sat down.

Darsk went back around his desk and sat down himself. The problem with Poncho was that he was short term, and Poncho knew it. The problem with McGuire was that he'd already failed the agency once and nobody was sure he wouldn't do it again. Darsk didn't trust the crazy illegal, but the bastard had guts. Hard to tell if Seamus still had an agent's moxie, or if pottery had rounded off all the edges.

———>●<———

Carmen fought off the Seconal in a few hours. She awoke disengaged, almost otherworldly, but strangely calm—the perfect state for the task at hand. In her drug-laced dreams she was 12, in a grand temple in India having dinner with her father and a Hindu mystic. The mystic was explaining the limitations of Western rationalism. He believed that the essential stuff of the universe was thinking non-stuff.

"The mind is not a projection of the brain as you in the West have taught," the mystic said. "Rather the other way around. The body is a projection of the mind."

"Ascending layers of consciousness are what is real," he instructed.

"The lowest center," he said, "is alimentary, for survival. Next, the sexual organs for procreation, then the stomach, the center of aggression, then the heart where spiritual transformation takes place."

"It's true," Bartholomew agreed. "All matter in the universe was once packed into a speck no bigger than an electron. All is space. Even particles are not there. They only appear to be there, and then, only when observed."

Carmen remembered her father was happy and laughing that night. "The world is a much wilder, much more fantastic place than we scientists ever imagined," he said, giving her a reassuring hug.

Carmen understood him now. Now she existed because she was observed. Like particles in space. Like pixels on a screen. Being an avatar was easy. She climbed the brownstone's main stairs, shaking loose her hair as she went. Clearing her mind of the drug. She entered the top floor studio and on one monitor set on local news there was an early report of two beautiful dogs found the night before with their throats slit.

"Oh my god," she said, "Seamus, where are you?"

She turned on the studio cameras and began shedding her clothes. She examined herself in the mirrored wall of the studio. Skinny, not just thin, she decided. Her cinnamon coloring was a drab whitish brown. It wasn't just the circles around her eyes but that her eyes looked lifeless. Flat like buttons, she thought. The MSG in the food. Too little air and too little light. She felt like a small mud puddle about to evaporate in the heat.

In a trance-like state, she loaded the feed of the massacre at Wide Waters into an external drive and queued it up for a special edition of *The Digital Darling Show*. She sat down naked and cross-legged on a giant red pillow in the middle of the stage. The rage drained from her body. She separated herself from all evil.

She was silent, but if you listened carefully, you could hear the sound of her deep measured breaths. After a few minutes she looked up into the camera, and said.

"I am Digital Darling and I love you."

Then she folded her hands together in reverence and began to chant.

At first her voice was barely audible, then it grew, emanating from deep inside her, gently ascending each internal layer. The groin, the gut, the heart, the brain. Her mantra became more fervent. She felt the vibrations take hold of one center after another, grasping consciousness, making her body as light as thought itself.

Then, without any physical effort beyond her melodious chant and the belief in her own particle weightlessness, she lifted herself above the cushion. She held herself aloft in a pure, lyrical moment of hope. Joseph's execrable footage backdropped her peacefulness. The studio was filled with sounds of conflict, screams of desperation, explosions and crackling gunfire.

———————

As if alerted by some new and powerful force nearby, Dave, crashed on the sofa downstairs, woke suddenly. It was 9 AM on his watch. He feared the house might be surrounded. He peeked through the window curtains but saw nothing unusual on Beacon Street or in the alley. He checked the kitchen and turned off the outside lights. Finding Carmen's bedroom empty, he rushed upstairs. He stood in the studio doorway paralyzed by the sight of her in mid air.

She was unaware of his presence. Suspended, she looked into the camera for the final time and said, "Tell me, Lord, how shall I serve?"

"Jesus," Dave uttered.

Transfixed, he never looked into the studio control room to see a small red warning light blinking at the bottom of the main panel. If he had, he would have realized that Carmen had forgotten to enter the routing sequence that guaranteed each broadcast passed through the untraceable router on the dark web.

They might as well have been broadcasting from Rockefeller Square.

Chapter 37
Free your mind

The petite brunette science director from the CDC pushed past the president's secretary the second she opened the door to the Oval Office.

"It's bees!" the high-strung CDC envoy said, handing North a thin report.

North looked up from the pile of papers on his desk. "Bumble bees?" he asked.

"No sir, deep jungle killer bees. They spread the deadly virus."

"The San Diego bug?" the president asked.

"Yes. ABPV to be precise. Acute Bee Paralysis Virus. The disease gets transferred to mites living in bee colonies. Naturally we targeted the planes' ventilation systems early on. We found dead bees, but it took time to discover they were carrying infected mites—that's what got released into the cabin."

"And breathed in by passengers?"

"Yes, Mr. President. Unfortunately, human lungs proved to be a perfect incubator for this particular retrovirus."

"All the bees are dead"

"Yes. We have the only samples remaining at the Center. The planes were quarantined and fumigated."

"That leaves the life cycle of the mites?" North asked, trying to understand.

"Exactly. We're studying that, Mr. President. Unfortunately, the relationship between the bees, these mites and the pollen has never been studied. We do believe the ABPV only spreads from the nest when the bees are busy gathering pollen. That cycle will be broken as soon the involved plants stop producing the pollen. A few more weeks."

"That's when the travel ban will end."

The CDC scientist slumped. "Should we advise the airline industry, Mr. President?"

"You've done your country a great service," North said. "Go back to Atlanta. Finalize your report. For now, keep those findings top secret. We'll make sure the Center understands the White House's position on this."

"Yes, Mr. President."

The president's secretary reappeared in the doorway. "It's Director Darsk again," she said. "He insists it's urgent."

Chapter 38
Top secret America

The night before Darsk ushered Seamus and Poncho into the windowless back room of the office and threatened that if both of them weren't still alive in the morning, he'd shoot whoever was left. Seamus took the cot and Poncho slept sitting up against the door.

Around dawn, the director barged through the door knocking Poncho to one side and waking both of them.

"We've got her," he said. "346 Beacon."

Seamus' heart sank.

"Take a piss. Wash your face. You got 30 seconds," Darsk ordered.

"McGuire," Darsk said, pointing at him when they were all back in the office a few minutes later, "Front door. Poncho, the alley. Nobody goes out. And you don't go in until I give the word."

Darsk was dialing the landline phone on his desk as he talked. "Yes, would you please tell the president that Director Darsk is calling and it's urgent," he said. Then looking up at Seamus and Poncho, "Don't even think about going in," he said, handing Seamus back his cell phone. "Move."

Seamus and Poncho hurried together down Fairfield toward Beacon Street. They could see from two blocks away the street had been barricaded. Boston cops were everywhere. As they walked, Seamus reached into his pocket and dialed the disposable cell phone mounted on the wall in the studio's control room. He texted 237867. CDRUNS.

As they approached the manned barricade at the corner of Beacon Street, Seamus said, "I'll take the cop on the right."

"O.K.," Poncho said, "I got leftie."

———————>●<———————

Unable to reach the president, Darsk had finally received Wilkins' blessing for the raid, when local cell networks, woefully overloaded by thousands of people downstreaming video, started to fail. Darsk frantically tried to reach the other members of the Boston NSA team but couldn't get through. He called Poncho and McGuire but had no luck. He got up and headed for Beacon Street, looking over and over at his watch. At Commonwealth Avenue he pulled out his gun to see if it was loaded and was suddenly stopped by two of Boston's finest.

"I'm the director of the NSA," Darsk protested.

The two cops looked at each other and laughed.

"Don't look familiar to me," said one officer.

"I'm a spy not a celebrity, you damn fool. You can't detain me."

"Actually," said the other cop, reaching under Darsk's coat and removing his gun, "we can."

Chapter 39
Bitch come running cologne

I f you ask far enough in advance and there's no competing event, the City of Boston will grant you a
parade permit. Thus did Digital Darling's burgeon-
ing Boston fan club receive permission to parade in her
honor. More specifically the right to assemble on Boston
Common and move down Beacon Street to Mass Ave.
and then disperse. The parade was coded B-level, that
is, 30 in uniform, six not, estimated crowd: up to 3000.
Timing for the parade, as the permit strictly noted, was
8 AM to 10 AM, on September 6th.

The very day of Carmen's on-screen ascension.

Her special edition of *The Digital Darling Show* had
gone viral. Clips of the show had made the morning talk
shows. The blogs were overwhelmed. There was even
news of a parade to be held in Boston today.

For the millions of fans who had traveled the world
with Digital Darling all summer her levitation was a tip-
ping point. She had at last taken on the most precious of
female vestiges—that of goddess. Many valued her spiritual guidance as much as her travel advice and instantly

embraced her miraculous act as proof of divine interven-
tion. She wasn't rising up from the earth. She was coming down from heaven. She deserved worship.

The religious community, which had stayed on the
sidelines of the Digital Darling affair until now, grasped
at the chance to bolster their own ministries. The Born
Agains led the way, followed quickly by Baptists,
Lutherans and Latter-Day Mormons. They got up from
their computers and TV screens in droves and headed
for Back Bay. The Teabaggers, Pentecostal Revivalists,
Modern Shakers, Abundant Life Christians, Fire for
Jesus worshippers and the Catacombs movement soon
got the message. The Willow Creekers, Little Wanderers
and three renegade sects of Catholicism supporting
Bishop Gaillot followed. George Barna understudies,
the Mennonite Council for Lesbian and Gay Concern,
media-starved groups like the National Suffering Project
and the Christian Laughter Movement, Sister Wendy
Beckett's followers and the Flirting for Jesus crowd also
implored their flocks to join the rally. They were bolstered
by a Pandora's box of broken souls who had turned to
electronic evangelism as a balm against the disappoint-
ment in their lives. Digital Darling had seduced not just
the travel-starved, but also chronic malcontents and the
karma-impaired. Psychics, remote viewers, the paranor-
mals shamans, those into astral travel, plus many more
who quietly believed they weren't born on this planet
in any event. They all got up, got dressed, and headed
for Boston Common. Many were genuinely moved by
Digital Darling's display of divinity, her virginal appear-

ance, her sheer boldness. Others were more enflamed by the unbounded commercial rewards of well-organized religion. When the rumor that many look-alikes might parade nude in total fealty to their goddess, thousands more regular folks called in late for work just for the chance to respectfully leer.

This unlikely assemblage emerged from the subway stops, flowed out of homes and offices, and snarled the rush hour traffic in lower Bay Back. The crowd goers proclaimed their allegiance, surrendered their souls, and swelled with pride. They carried makeshift signs—*Holy Mother of God, Rapture Now, Tribulation to Non-Believers, Jesus is A Woman, Segrado Madre*—and chanted these slogans in rolling succession. They held their Blackberries, Droids and iPhones overhead, filming, broadcasting, commanding the country's attention. They demanded so much bandwidth they brought cell service in the entire metropolitan area down.

Boston's Metropolitan Police were hastily reinforced by their mounted corps, available state troopers and MBTA officials. Together, they managed to clear the Common and Garden and surrounding streets with loudspeakers, horses and threatening nightsticks. The crowd, now estimated in the tens of thousands, surged onto lower Beacon Street. Look-alikes, believing themselves symbiotically blessed, formed a phalanx at the head of the parade, several stripping themselves naked in a final act of submission.

Their nakedness only added to the frenzy.

Mobile media vans were on the job. One perky blonde

reporter who might have passed for Digital Darling herself, attempted to explain the building chaos. "There are unconfirmed reports from Internet bloggers," she said, "that a series of recent deaths, including several people in Maine, as well as James Holliston, vice president of the State Street Bank here in Boston, are part of a government effort to squash the Digital Darling movement. Local officials deny these reports, but as you can see and hear behind me, this is a highly charged demonstration."

The true believers pressed up Beacon Street, cheered on by residents who had gathered on the sidewalks and rooftops down both sides of the parade route. Hundreds more hung out of windows urging the multitude on.

———◦◦◦———

Seamus approached the officer on the right and said, "See that Mexican over there? He's carrying a gun."

A ferocious scuffle ensued. It took the two burly cops almost five minutes to beat Poncho into semi-consciousness. They threw him into the back of their squad car.

Poncho woke up in the screened-in, handle-less back seat. It seemed to him that Seamus should be in the back seat, too. His heels soon ached from trying to kick out the shatterproof windows.

———◦◦◦———

The parade, which had grown rowdy before it left the park, turned ugly just as it reached Fairfield Street. A young policeman furious after being knocked to the ground and nearly trampled to death responded with pepper spray. He blanketed a large section of the marchers, indiscriminately blinding adults, teenagers and babies in carriers. The sounds of children screaming in pain awakened the parade-goers' revolutionary roots. Some were boomers, veteran protestors. They had been on the streets in the 60s. They remembered Attica and Waco. They were weaned on Vietnam. They were tired of big business, big government and big lies. They were losing their personal freedoms, their standard of living, their hope. They were getting fucked and they knew it. If Digital Darling had the guts to say so, so did they. They started by flattening street signs and throwing rocks and whatever else was handy at the cops.

Or at cop cars.

Poncho ducked as a brick bent in the side window just enough for him to pull it out of its tracks.

"There is plenty of blame to go around here in Boston," one nervous reporter on the scene began. "Some predicted this parade's riot potential." He shoved his microphone in the face of one passer-by. "Why are you here?"

"People want to know," the young man said. "What do they owe a dishonest government?"

"But isn't this about religion?" the reporter asked.

"Politics, religion," the parader said. "It's about duty."

Another intrepid reporter and his cameraman had climbed to relative safety atop a parked truck to continue broadcasting.

"You will recall that the American Revolution began here in Boston," the gray-haired female reporter from PBS said. "Local officials aren't commenting on that irony, or on the widespread challenge to authority that is transpiring here. It is clear, however, that Americans, at least those here in the nation's first colony, have had enough. Given the remarkable display of loyalty to Digital Darling, there is no doubt they have had quite enough of the President North's ban on travel, and who knows what else."

———>●<———

Dave and Carmen had reacted immediately to the coded message from Seamus. CDRUNS: Carmen Dave RUN Seamus. The R also meant use the roof.

Dave rushed upstairs to set the studio on "fry everything." Carmen hastily fed the paperwork into the blazing living room fireplace. They grabbed two bags packed at the beginning of summer for just such an eventuality. They could hear someone kicking at the kitchen door and the sound of breaking wood as they exited through the roof garden.

They ran down the long row of townhouses to Gloucester Street. They took a fire escape to the ground. As the parade passed by out front, they slipped into the melee. Carmen blended into the sea of look-alikes.

"Seamus is alive," she said hopefully, as the rabble-rousers carried them along.

"He's a Fed," Dave said.

"But he warned us," Carmen argued.

"Just don't take your clothes off," Dave begged her.

A car was waiting for them at Mass Ave. with a ride to Hanscom Field. They rode in silence over the Charles River toward Cambridge, Carmen glowering out the side window at the steadfast domes of MIT.

Part Three

"What I would love
is to have any boy
in the world who thinks
of pirates to think of...
Disney pirates."

– Robert Iger, president, The Walt Disney Company

Third interrogation
Quantitative easing

The interrogation room seemed smaller every time Seamus walked into it.

The questioning had gone on for nearly three weeks. Today, the guy across the table was new. Maybe Seamus had worn out the others. He was beat, too.

"Every decision, McGuire. Every opportunity," the interrogator said, pawing through the file, "you took the wrong turn."

"I'm a good spy," Seamus said. "Just appeared that way."

"First a potter, now a comedian." The man got up, probably so he could look down on Seamus. He was large, middle-aged and humorless. Like most special agents, there was nothing special about him.

"Somewhere around a 35 share, everyone in a hissy-fit, and you're sitting on your ass?" The man leaned down over Seamus, "And plugging hers."

Seamus wanted to smack him.

"You need to wake up, McGuire. Start showing some respect. Maybe your employer would have a little compassion for you."

That sounded like an offer, Seamus thought, the first sign they were willing to compromise.

"And when push came to shove," the interrogator said, "you made a cell call to 346 Beacon."

That brought Seamus up short. Absolutely nothing is private anymore. His expression gave him away.

"Didn't think we had that, huh?" the interrogator bragged. "Enough to hang you right there."

Seamus took a deep breath.

"Let's get this over with, McGuire. Where the fuck are they?"

Seamus didn't blink. "I have absolutely no idea," he said. "They didn't tell me everything."

The agent's cell phone rang and he answered it.

"Yeah," he said. "He's right here...what? McGuire? All respect, director, sure you got that right?"

The man looked over at Seamus in disbelief.

"The president wants to see you," the interrogator said, dumbfounded.

"Lunch?" Seamus said cheerfully.

"I don't believe it," the man said, tossing his phone on the table. "They're gonna give you some goddam award."

Chapter 40
The happiest
place on earth

Barely able to contain his glee, Pipes Barronson leaned back in his desk chair, put his hands behind his head and watched the noon news. The Associated Press put it this way:

"Cinderella, Snow White and Tinker Bell were handcuffed, frisked and loaded into police vans today as a labor protest brought a touch of reality to the Happiest Place on Earth.

"In all, 32 protesters, most of them wearing costumes representing well-known Disney characters, were arrested. As they were taken into custody wearing plastic handcuffs, hundreds of fellow theme park and hotel workers cheered, chanted and brandished signs that read, *Shame on Mickey* and *F**k The Duck*.

"Bewildered tourists fled the scene as picketers protesting pay cuts and reduced health care benefits, closed the rides at California Adventure for three hours. The fictional childhood characters were charged with a misdemeanor.

"Disney representatives commented that, given the

extraordinary strain placed on resort properties during the travel ban, the union's position was not only unreasonable, it was 'hopeless.'"

"Happiest place on earth my snow white ass!" Barronson shouted out on his way to North's office.

⟫⟫◆◄⟪

Earlier that same morning, North had met with Ms. Navaho for an update on the entertainment empire. It wasn't all whistling while you work. Euro Disney faltered. An attempt to move into China also had problems, as had an attempt to open a marine theme park in Long Beach. A bid to bring history alive in rural Virginia called *Disney America*, and *Celebration*, which answered the question how many people wanted to live in a Norman Rockwell painting, both lost their luster. A new pro football team, a series of missteps in video sports; and learning vacations under the title, *Disney Institute* were all trashed. Billions in losses had obliterated the conglomerate's bottom line three years running. The ban had to be killing them.

As bad, Disney had a religious problem. Outraged over the release of adult-content movies under the Miramax label, the Southern Baptists rallied everyone from the American Family Association to scary splinter groups like the Rapturists to lead a dogged worldwide boycott of Disney operations. To be sure, Disney was still an entertainment behemoth. It controlled enough media outlets to sway the public discourse in America and sixteen international digital channels anxiously awaited native-speaking Mickeys, Donalds, Goofys and Cinderellas of their own. Plus there was all the high-margin commemorative merchandise anyone could carry home. Simply put, Disney Inc. had more influence than the US State Department, a conviction it spent millions each year promoting.

The corporation's defiance had been the biggest burr under North's saddle since the travel ban began. Plus, he needed the entertainment giant intact.

Barronson breezed into the oval office.

"You're going to love this, Mr. President," he said, clicking through channels on the president's TV until he found a live broadcast from Anaheim.

"Bewildered tourists in Disney t-shirts and caps, some pushing strollers gawked at the costumed picketers getting hauled away," an on-scene reporter said.

Then, interviewing one on-looker, "It's changing my opinion of Disneyland," said Ms. Amanda Kosto who was visiting from Melbourne, Australia. "This really stinks."

"Sit tight," the president said to Pipes. He pushed a button on his intercom and asked his secretary to get Wisener on the phone.

The chairman of Disney took his call poolside in Miami Beach.

"We can be on the same team," North said immediately.

Wisener listened as the president outlined nothing less than the grandest public-private partnership ever. A Constitution rattling co-op that would control a sizeable portion of the nation's economy.

"Imagine everyone in the country carrying a travel ID card with a picture of Mickey on it. Imagine an embedded chip on that card capturing every transaction," North said.

"Twenty-five percent," Wisener said, after the briefest pause.

"We own most of what you don't," North replied. "We've already begun compiling the data."

"You need Disney to commercialize that data, Mr. President. But I'm sympathetic to the country's financial posture. Twenty percent."

"Twelve," North said. "I've seen the midday news."

"Fifteen, and I'll look forward to a prompt lifting of the ban," Wisener bargained.

There was a pause on both sides.

Finally Wisener, feeling that his silence had started to convey weakness more than resolve, spoke up. "One thing, Alex," he said. "No hard feelings, OK?"

Back in the oval office, North and Barronson swapped fist pumps.

Chapter 41
Too big to fail

The president gathered his inner circle beneath the West Wing in the Situation Room. Wilkins, Darsk, Barronson and Ms. Navaho were all there. North didn't hide his news or his excitement.

"We have Disney," he said.

Ms. Navaho's eyebrows went up.

"Due largely to your efforts," North reassured her. "Wisener finally saw our side of it. Besides, we needed him solvent. He realized that and it was the right time to make a deal."

"Let's recap," North said. "If I'm quoting you correctly, madam secretary, the desire to travel outranks the desire to spend time with family and friends, pursue a healthier way of life, and after about age 45, it evens outranks the desire to have sex." The commerce secretary blushed.

"I'm suggesting," the president said. "We've been in the wrong business."

"Not thinking of turning the reflecting pool into Aquaboggin, are you, Mr. President?" Wilkinson said with a grin.

North remained effervescent. "What's the greatest thing about this country?" he asked. "Is it still the land of opportunity? Or only if you can get financing? Personal freedom? Or did that disappear with the Patriot Acts?"

"There are still places to hide," Wilkins said.

"Damn few," North replied. "I believe the greatest thing about this country is its natural beauty. Our Grand Canyon is the world's deepest. Yellowstone is the greatest concentration of geo-thermal phenomena anywhere. Our giant redwoods are the world's tallest trees. Big Sur has been rightly called the finest meeting of land and sea anywhere on the planet. Peaks. Plains. Caverns. Cliffs. We've got it all. Plus we've got man-made splendor— Washington D.C., right here, has more museums and monuments than any city in the world. We've got Las Vegas, Times Square, two major Disneys, plus thousands of theme parks and roadside attractions. The whole darn country is a tourist attraction."

"Everybody wants to come here as it is," Darsk said, referring largely to illegal immigration problems.

"No they don't," North said. "We're second to France in visitors. A country one-twentieth our size. And Spain and China are right on our butt."

"Spain?" Wilkins asked.

"Don't underestimate Spain. Three years ago, they were second," Ms. Navaho said, "and we were third."

"Worse," North said. "We haven't sold our own people. Nine out of every ten Americans would rather visit a foreign country than see more of this country."

"What exactly have you got in mind, Mr. President?"

Pipes asked.

"Listen," North said. "Add up our national and state parks, town parks, thousands of historic places and designated areas. Think about the Native American territories as destinations. Hell, we've been printing commemorative currency for years. But it's all been peanuts up until now. While the ban has been in effect we've taken control of half the country's privately owned tourist attractions. What we don't have is a cabinet-level department of tourism."

"Neither does France," Wilkins said.

"France isn't bankrupt," North said firmly. "We have to get beyond encouraging tourism, and start making money on it. Lots of money."

North hadn't shared the grand scale of his plan with any of them until now, even Wilkins. He considered the worried looks on the faces of his small audience. The chief of staff worried it would never get through Congress. Darsk was concerned about who would control it. Ms. Navaho feared that every citizen would end up dependent on federal government just like Native Americans were already. Pipes visualized the inflammatory headlines sure to follow.

North played his trump card.

"Civilizations, the great ones, become living museums," North said patiently. "All societies fail. That is the way history unfolds. We can sit around and cry about it, or we can make a fortune on the ruins."

Chapter 42
Alienation nation

Seamus, Poncho and Darsk stood at attention in the great room of North's western White House, centerpiece of the sprawling Triple H Ranch in the high country north of Sedona, Arizona. The president was pinning Legion of Merit awards on each of their chests. One of Barronson's minions was videotaping the small ceremony. The First Lady was playing *America the Beautiful* on the piano.

Seamus worried he was going to end up on the evening news, something Carmen might see. Or in some database Dave might eventually discover. Where they might be hiding was never off his mind.

"I want to congratulate the three of you," North was saying. "Director Darsk, you've shown the kind of forbearance and ingenuity that make the NSA integral to the security of our country. Agent Poncho, I understand your courageous undercover work led directly to those who were behind this conspiracy. Despite risks to your personal safety."

Poncho threw his shoulders back another inch.

The president turned to Seamus. "Agent McGuire, your reports from inside the underground studio have been invaluable in putting this matter to rest. The kind of smart work I wish we had more of."

Seamus tried to keep his eyes from rolling back in his head. Darsk's report must have read like an episode of *24 Hours*. The truth was so managed at the top that facts were irrelevant.

If they were getting the credit, Seamus wondered who would take the fall.

"The director tells me you've been with the agency for some time," North said to Seamus.

"Not all of it active, sir," Seamus replied.

"Some misunderstanding along our southern border?"

Misunderstanding? Shooting illegals along the border for fun? I'm sure the Mexicans misunderstood why bullets were ripping through their bodies.

"Yes, sir, a misunderstanding," was all Seamus could say.

"Wouldn't have happened in my administration," North said. "No need to be shooting desperate people. Glad you had the courage to resist those orders."

Maybe this guy wasn't so bad after all, Seamus thought. Anyway, he was getting off the hook.

Poncho looked over at Seamus and managed a thin smile. A grudging sign of respect.

The president stepped back from the unlikely love fest to survey his work. He pushed Seamus and Poncho together for the camera like they were Starsky and Hutch.

"Darsk has plans for both of you. We've already talked…"

"Actually, sir—" Seamus began.

"You'll go over that with Darsk," North said, cutting him off. "For now, you should know that your efforts have saved us precious resources and time…you've helped dramatically shorten our ban on travel."

Poncho swelled up. The improbable life path that had started on the border just a couple hundred miles south had led right into the president's home. Some country, this America. Patriotism pulsed through his veins. He looked forward to exterminating more undesirables.

"What about Digital Darling," Seamus said. "Carmen Brand?"

"There's no current effort to bring her in," Darsk interjected.

"Exactly," North said. "No sense making a martyr of her."

Seamus was relieved but deflated. He wondered where Carmen was and if she cared where he was.

"Gentlemen, if you'll excuse me," North said. "Director, I'll leave it to you and the chief of staff. Again, your country thanks you. Congratulations."

Darsk saluted as the president left the room.

Eliza picked it up on the piano.

Chapter 43
Desert Storm

Wilkins' meeting with Darsk after the ceremony was brief and blunt.

"The Department of Commerce will take the lead, but the president wants the agency present on each reservation during their changeover to major destinations. I know you're not entirely onboard with this, but the reservations can be big moneymakers. We need to put a face on that besides an illegal immigrant, so McGuire got lucky. I understand he knows the Hopi, speaks some of the language."

"That's right."

"Good. Drop him off at Orabai. Station Poncho with the Navahos."

"Actually, Bob, Mexicans and Native Americans..."

"I'm aware of the racial pecking order here in America, director. Just station the Mexican in New Mexico. That work for you?"

"I suppose."

"The president would appreciate no supposes on this. He wants your personal involvement." Wilkins closed the folder on his desk, rose and shook Darsk's hand.

"We're not taking the damn reservations back, Frank," he said. "We're helping the tribes develop them. There's no wringing of hands in the White House over this. It's not all rich Massapequas out there. We can't make it skimming gambling profits."

"But these two?"

"Hell, if these aren't the guys...maybe they have to leave the program. Poncho wasn't yours to start with. McGuire's convenient, but there's no crowd around him either. Have I made myself clear?"

Darsk nodded. He didn't know how many tape recorders and cameras were hidden in the room, so he tightened his grip on Wilkins' hand to say he understood what the chief of staff meant: they were expendable.

—————⟫●⟪—————

Poncho was outside leaning up against the wall, near the open window where Darsk and Wilkins were talking. He was chewing on some sage grass, listening to every word.

When he was growing up in the tough neighborhoods of east LA, Poncho learned that you're only vulnerable when you're not in control. And the worse way to be out of control is to have to trust someone.

Chapter 44
Rare, but serious
side effects

R oute 40 east of Flagstaff stretched across a high desert plain routinely buffeted by a steady wind, and the government-issued SUV jerked constantly to the right despite Poncho's firm grip on the steering wheel. Seamus was in the rear seat and Darsk rode shotgun. Signs for the Meteor City Trading Post passed by—Kachina Dolls and Pottery For Sale, Injun Town, then Geronimo Slept Here. And here. Exits pointed to Tonto National Bridge, Humphrey's Peak, the Painted Desert and Zane Grey's cabin. Poncho squinted in the early morning sun. It was going to be another hot windy day in northern Arizona.

Just beyond Winslow, Poncho turned left onto Route 87 and entered Indian Territory. They would first drop Seamus off with the Hopi, then head east to New Mexico. Hopiland was contained entirely within the Navaho reservation, 100 miles north. The two–lane blacktop road extended as far as the eye could see, flanked by only an occasional ramshackle homestead and a lone horse or cow grazing the open land. All signs of commercialism quickly disappeared. Hawks and vultures sailed over-head. Otherwise there was no sign of life, or water.

Darsk was explaining how it was going to be. He enthusiastically shared the president's vision for a more self-sufficient, fiscally responsible America. The NSA would provide boots on the ground as the Department of Commerce transformed the country's Indian reserva-tions into full-blown national parklands. Tribes would eventually benefit from billions in government devel-opment. Mobile homes and army salvage Quonset huts would be replaced by plush condominiums. First-class tourist destinations with spas, swimming pools, racetracks and casinos would dot the now desolate land. Roads would be improved. Broadband would be installed. People with money to spend would come. Every Native American would finally be brought into the main stream of national well-being.

"Anybody asked the tribes about this?" Seamus asked, already knowing the answer.

"Reservations are the most rancid stretches of pov-erty left in the country," Darsk countered. "They're blighted with rotted-out homes and toxic sewage. Believe me, they'll welcome our help."

"Government helped them before—"

"Don't be so fucking cynical, McGuire," Darsk said angrily, turning around to glare at Seamus.

"Money always helps," Poncho said.

"That's the attitude," Darsk agreed. "Just look at that horse over there," he said pointing out the window. "Looks half dead. Money buys feed grain." Then, "We need gas?"

"The only station is at Second Mesa," Seamus offered. "A few miles up."

Poncho pressed down on the accelerator and the SUV flew over the empty rolling roadway. Suicidal tumbleweeds crossed their path but little else. Hours later they reached the intersection of Route 264 at the foot of Second Mesa. There was a post office, Indian Arts shop and a Shell station that sold gasoline, propane and, according to a large sign, ran a livestock auction out back. The intersection was deserted.

Poncho pulled around to the rear of the Shell station near the corrals. When Darsk questioned why, Poncho turned toward him and smiled. The kind of smile a Mexican offers when he's either hurt, or he's about to hurt you. Slowly, Poncho withdrew a 45-caliber pistol from under his shirt and pointed it at his boss.

Chapter 45
The sound of automatic weapon fire

Seamus was out of the car before Darsk's brains finished splattering against the passenger-side window.

He ran for the corral and mounted an unsaddled pinto standing motionless in the hot sun. He hunched over the horse's neck and kicked him hard. They went out the open gate and quickly disappeared into the low scrub pines and high sagebrush of the surrounding desert.

Poncho stood with his hands on his hips and watched Seamus go. "He woulda done the same to you, amigo," he said, disappointed that Seamus was now a problem, too.

Poncho went around the SUV and pulled Darsk from the car. He hoisted the body up into the station's rusted Dumpster, and without bothering to clean up the mess inside turned the vehicle west on Route 264. In a few miles, the pavement climbed the switchbacks on the eastern slope of Second Mesa. Part way up he pulled over at a lookout. Far above him, the Hopi pueblos atop the mesa were reputed to be the oldest continuously occupied spot in North America. Poncho understood why. Even half-way up, the mesa provided an unobstructed view of the seamless flatlands that stretched for hundreds of miles in all directions. Perfect protection against an advancing enemy.

Poncho surveyed the landscape. Several hundred yards below he could see the dust trail of a lone rider on horseback.

———⟫●⟪———

Seamus saw the sand explode before he heard the retort of the rifle. A second blast tore through a nearby aloe bush. He jerked the horse left and rode it hard toward the large rocks at the base of the mesa. He dismounted, and slapped the horse's rump to send it on its way. He hoped Poncho wouldn't shoot it just for fun. Except for a screeching hawk riding the updraft along the cliffs, the desert remained quiet.

Seamus scrambled up the rocks and situated himself about 30 feet above the desert floor. Protected from above by an overhang, he had a clear view of the trail for a long way east and south. He pulled the agency revolver from his shoulder holster, checked the clip and counted ten rounds. He flipped the safety off.

Using a piece of quartz rock he found nearby, he scraped some grey sandstone off one large rock, spit into the dust to make a paste, then rubbed it on his cheekbones and forehead. Finally, he turned down the yellow lining on his shirtsleeves.

He sat Indian style, cross-legged, straight-backed,

every sense on alert. An hour passed. He didn't move his head as his eyes scanned the horizon, to the left, then right and slowly back again. Without moving his upper body, he occasionally stretched his legs for circulation, first one then the other, in a controlled yoga-like fashion.

The sun dipped below the top edge of the mesa high above him, covering his position in the shadows, then shrouding rock after rock below. He watched the sun draw a dark retreating line that approached then enveloped the trail. Poncho would be along soon.

Out of the corner of one eye—a brief reflection in the retreating sun. And what might be the swirling dust of a vehicle coming to a halt. He thought he saw something scurrying among the cacti, but on second take it was a family of prairie dogs. Maybe someone scared them. Closer and to his right, a sidewinder slithered by.

Seamus rolled forward on his haunches and made a cradle with his body: right elbow on the inside of the right knee, upper left arm atop the left knee. He gripped his weapon firmly against his cheekbone, pressing hard enough to make him squint. He pushed some moss into his left ear to protect his hearing, and then rocked back and forth finding the exact point of equilibrium. Take a deep breath. Sight. Steady. Squeeze. Just like they taught him. No hesitation. No second thoughts about killing a Mexican this time.

———⇒●⇐———

At home in the gullies and washes, long-addicted to risk, Poncho was on the move. He crawled and wormed his way toward the base of the mesa where the horse had exited. He used the greasewood and eucalyptus and sage-brush and even tumbleweed as cover. The late afternoon shadows cast by a large stand of saguaro gave him cour-age. When he stopped at the far side of the trail, he was less than a hundred yards from the tumbled down rocks.

———————⟫●⟪———————

Suddenly all hell broke loose with bullets ricochet-ing off the rocks over Seamus' head. Then another volley, lower and to his right. Poncho was on a fishing trip.

The pop-pop-pop was all too familiar—standard issue US Army M-16. Seamus went over what he could remember about the automatic assault weapon:

Bullets leave the barrel so quickly they don't spiral they tumble. When they hit, they don't just pierce the flesh, they ravage the body, shattering bones, which in turn become deadly projectiles flying apart in all direc-tions, ripping through organs, veins and muscles and tissue. Massive bleeding was the intended result— taking the victim's insides with the exiting bullets. The M-16 wasn't accurate over distances, but no weapon wreaked more havoc at close range. Compact and light-weight, it could empty a 60-round clip in three seconds. It could level a whole company of charging men. It was the perfect weapon if you weren't sure what you were aiming at. It had been perfect for Vietnam.

Seamus blinked repeatedly and broke into a sweat, but managed to sit still. He squinted to minimize the chances for even a slight reflection. Fuck. Where'd

Poncho get that?

The former stunt man hadn't spotted him yet, but this was going to be a lot more one-sided than Seamus hoped.

He sat very still until the sun finally set.

A pale harvest moon, low at first on the horizon, came up overhead, casting a cool gray light across the abandoned land. Bats swooped by. A desert owl glided gracefully along the edge of the mesa. A slew of spiders and night feeders crawled by. Dozens of brown mice, carriers of the dreaded hantavirus, scurried around him, squeaking. Occasionally, he could see the lights of a vehicle pass by far in the distance. As the night wore on, fatigue began to erode his concentration and resolve. He was haunted by something the service had taught him: The person with the advantage in combat is the one most willing to die. It wasn't a comforting thought. The chill of the desert night crept into his bones, but kept him awake.

———⇒⋗●⋖⇐———

Poncho had spent plenty of nights in worse places and had managed a few hours sleep. Like a predator who feeds in the morning, he welcomed the day's first light. He pushed a fresh clip into the M-16 and drove a round home. He stretched and spit. Stupid potter, he said to himself, who did he think he was fuckin' with?

———⇒⋗●⋖⇐———

Seamus moved. Hardly at all. Just enough to rub the dust and sleep from his eyes.

In a flash, bullets were pinging off the rocks all

around him. He dove into a deep crevice behind some greasewood and kept crawling. The pop-pop-pop of the M-l6 followed him down. One bullet ricocheted off the rocks and caught him in the shoulder. He heard something crack. He almost lost consciousness with the first wave of pain. Instinctively, he reached for his shattered collarbone as if to hold it together. Part way down the rocks he paused to gather himself and took up a position between two large boulders that afforded a slim vertical view of the wash on the far side of the road.

He could see Poncho coming, zigzagging between the stately cacti.

Seamus fired twice and took the top off one saguaro as Poncho dashed by. But the .45 wasn't accurate at this range and his adversary knew it.

Poncho broke into the clear, the M-16 mounted at his hip, spraying more rounds in Seamus' direction.

Seamus felt a second bullet enter his thigh and tear away the flesh as it exited. He lost hold of his handgun and watched it bounce down the rocks below him. Unsure how to deal with the pain, he rolled back onto the flat rock behind him and looked up the face of the mesa at Second Oraibi. Standing on a small outcrop a hundred feet above he could make out the familiar outline of his blood brother, Chosposi. Home from his road show due to the ban, Seamus presumed. Had someone discovered Darsk's body behind the station? Had Chosposi tracked him into the desert and waited all night for the right moment?

Seamus gave him the traditional Hopi open-handed

salute but got no response. Then he took a chance. He struggled onto his good leg and stood up, managing to get both hands in the air.

"You're a government agent," he reminded Poncho at the top of his lungs.

Poncho stepped from behind a saguaro where he'd paused to un-jam the M-16.

"I resigned yesterday," he said with a big grin.

Suddenly the lone shot of a powerful rifle echoed across the empty desert. Poncho clutched his chest and fell to his knees.

———⟫●⟪———

When Seamus opened his eyes, Chosposi was stuffing eucalyptus leaves into tattered flesh of his wounds. The Hopi chief gave him a drink from a potion of desert flowers and pain-relieving mushrooms he always carried with him.

Nearby, Poncho lived awhile longer. Chosposi knelt over him and held his head above the sand.

"I am dying," Poncho said. "This time for real."

Chosposi nodded. "I will bury you."

"Bury me deep," Poncho said, managing a grin. "Or I will crawl out."

"He will disappear," Chosposi said to Seamus some time later. "He will be treated with respect."

Indian respect for one's enemies, Seamus recalled.

Chosposi tied a rawhide tourniquet around Seamus' leg, and then lifted his bloody friend onto his horse. He gave Seamus a flat-lipped stare.

"How do I look?" Seamus asked.

"Better last time," the Indian said.

Seamus passed out.

Chapter 46
Eco-magic

President Alexander North stood on the west stairway of the White House behind a bank of microphones and a live audience of several hundred insiders. He was about to become the most popular man in America.

He began slowly, unfurling an exquisite list of benefits stemming from his often-criticized ban on travel: Everything from crime to divorce rates was down. Illness, court cases, absenteeism, juvenile delinquency, even public profanity were all in retreat. Credit card balances had been reduced, too. People were saving for college, retirement and significant holidays rather than just buzzing aimlessly around. Sensible Americans were fixing up their homes and yards and getting to know their neighbors and spouses and kids.

Admittedly, some of the good news was a projection of Pipes' fertile imagination, but it all sounded true. Mother Nature, the president claimed, had been given a full season to herself to recuperate. Fish were returning to long-barren streams, bears and mountain lions to the timberline, grass to the country's many parks. Indoors, the performing arts were enjoying a revival. Contributions to non-profits were on the rise. Courtesy had returned to the nation's streets. Fewer accidents, traffic jams, and incidents of road rage. Air pollution figures were down, as were noise pollution and pressure on landfills. The number of mood-altering drug prescriptions backed off record highs, as did visits to psychiatrists, psychologists, and an assemblage of unlicensed counselors and outright gladhanders. Household pets were better behaved, so North claimed. And without a doubt, with millions of gallons of jet fuel going unused and automobile travel way off, the price of gas at the pump had mercifully declined. Everyone was touched by the price of gas. Public confidence in the general state of affairs was downright rosy.

It was a win-win-win speech and North smiled broadly throughout his presentation. Things were good and they were about to get even better.

There was, of course, no mention that a government agency supposedly dedicated to protecting the populace from foreign enemies had burned a distinguished citizen's private home to the ground, killed dozens of innocent people, sealed the files of the whole affair under a national security label, and moved on. No acknowledgement of the Boston riots, or that Director Darsk had never found Digital Darling, or Carmen Brand, or whoever. Instead, Pipes cast the entire affair in terms of war with an identifiable, beatable enemy—killer bees.

North spread his arms in his characteristic grand embrace and winked into the edifying late afternoon sunlight. "Ladies and gentlemen," he said to those gathered, "our ability to solve the problems before us is unquestioned."

The reporters leaned forward and the cameras hummed.

The president continued. "Our Center for Disease Control has informed me that the control measures we put in place have been successful. I want to congratulate the American people for their forbearance and patriotism. Our beleaguered business community. Our stalwart Congress. I am delighted to announce to you today that the ban on travel and tourism is lifted—effective immediately."

The president threw up his hands in triumph and members of the White House staff and selected Congressional supporters crowded the steps around him in backslapping, hand-shaking congratulations.

━━━━━━━━━━━

Across the country a cheer rose up. From kitchen tables, media rooms, and city condo roof decks. From a million lunch counters and trading desks. Up from behind the empty hotel concierge stands and from inside the near-abandoned corridors of the nation's airports. The cheer was carried over the web, by word-of-mouth, by the wind itself. It was propelled by a sense of shared misfortune now lifted. Spread by the force of communal love, it was the joyous, unmistakable sound of freedom.

In the days that followed, the president basked in approval ratings that set records. Americans coast to coast called their lonely travel agents to re-book.

North rode the wave. At night he dreamed of red ink washing away by the gallon.

Curiosity about the animatronic super-human called Digital Darling burned out like a meteorite, her memory preserved by a small band of devotees.

Sales of Digital Darling Ware dropped precipitously, and before long, all but disappeared.

Chapter 47
String theory

C armen awoke to the ominous swooshing sound of a Bell 206 helicopter as it set down in the small backyard of the hideaway Dave had arranged for her in Key West.

Ten minutes later, she and Ms. Navaho were staring at each other over iced tea in the cottage's Florida room.

Carmen spoke first.

"So Seamus was a spy?"

"We prefer agent."

"You interrogated him," Carmen asked.

"We did."

"He betrayed us?"

"If by 'us,' you mean your country, then yes," Ms. Navaho replied.

"Are you saying he didn't betray me and my father?"

The commerce secretary leaned forward but ignored Carmen's question. "Everyone wants something from his or her country," she said. "You, for instance, want to be left alone. I can arrange that, but first here's something you can help us with, Ms. Brand. We're missing another agent besides Seamus, and our NSA director has been murdered. Naturally, this is an urgent matter."

"You don't know where they are, do you?"

"In Hopiland."

"Big territory. Full of Indians."

"I'm speaking for our president, Ms. Brand. Go to Seamus. When he tells you what happened to Director Darsk and agent Poncho, you tell us. And it ends."

"Like you ended things with my father?"

"Seamus can be tried for treason. Does that matter to you?"

"He's gone. I'm off the air. Doesn't that solve your problem?"

The secretary leaned back and laughed. "Frankly, we'd love to think so."

"Isn't democracy supposed to thrive on public debate?" Carmen shot back.

"It wasn't possible to be as transparent as the president would have preferred."

"So my father was right. The travel ban was bullshit."

"There were large forces at work here, Ms. Brand. Forces that threatened our country as a whole."

"Would one of those forces be the truth?"

"Our side of the story is the truth. You understand, any public comment to the contrary by you or Seamus and the deal ends, badly."

Carmen got up and moved around the room to better gauge how hard her arm was being twisted. "Big helicopter," she mused, looking out the window.

"I'm offering you a ride," Ms. Navaho said cheerfully.

Carmen didn't want to go anywhere. She wished Dave were there.

"President North feels strongly that an armed agency presence in Indian Territory right now would be counter-productive. The NSA's desire for a more vigorous investigation, therefore, has taken a back seat to the president's wish to convert our nation's *peaceful* reservations into *safe* tourist attractions."

"I don't know," Carmen said.

"I'll accompany you to Oraibi," the secretary continued. "When they find out who you are, they'll take you to him. You're mistaken if you think the offers get better. Besides, Seamus has been seriously wounded."

Carmen turned around suddenly. "How do you know that if you're not sure where he is?"

"We found you didn't we?"

Carmen let out a sigh. There was no way to trust these people. No way to ignore them. Suppose Seamus was really hurt? Suppose the secretary was actually trying to do her a favor?

"I'll need to pack a few things," Carmen said.

Ms. Navaho smiled. "You'll see that doing the right thing for your country works out for the best. I'll never understand why people find that possibility so unlikely."

The secretary stood up and extended her hand to shake. "Is Dave here?" she asked.

"Dave who?" Carmen said.

———⟫●⟪———

Eleven hours later, after refueling in Houston, the

Department of Commerce helicopter touched down right in front of the Shell station where Darsk's body had been recovered by the agency the week before.

The secretary reached forward and opened the chopper door for Carmen. As Carmen rose to leave, the secretary put her hand on her arm. She gave Carmen a no-nonsense look. "Watch your step," she advised.

Chapter 48
Hopiland

A t first, the Hopi women showed Carmen how to brew a healing tea from wild mint, make soup from dandelions and pain relievers from creosote bushes. It was how they had nursed Seamus, and the next day they took an anxious Carmen to him.

She woke him with a kiss and when he tried to speak she gently pressed her finger to his lips. She never left his side and within a week had him sitting up and smiling. In two weeks he was strong enough for Carmen to make love to him. A week later they borrowed two ponies and took a leisurely ride into the desert.

Carmen had changed, too. On horseback, she wore a colorful handcrafted cotton skirt gathered at the waist by a tooled leather belt. On top she wore a leather-fringed cotton shirt. Black and yellow beads had been weaved into her long hair.

Seamus stared at her as if for the first time. Gone were the sharp, frantic edges of their electronic life on Beacon Street. The darting eyes, the twitching at night as she slept. She was the country girl who had approached his van in search of pots. Warm, peaceful, and unafraid.

"Chosposi has offered to make us partners," he said to her that day. "He will sponsor you as he did me."

"Is that a proposal, Mr. Potterman?"

"If you believe as the Hopi do that marriage is a spiritual union," Seamus said. "There is a ceremony, and a difficult challenge," he explained. "Chosposi would be honored if you chose him as your sponsor. I would be honored if you said yes."

Carmen beamed.

———————

The next morning when Seamus awoke, Carmen was gone. Then rarely seen for several days.

She was being passed among the village elders for instruction. She learned that the word, "Hopi" meant peace, that the purpose of her initiation ceremony was to maintain harmony with the universe, and that the purpose of life was to become ready for inner change. She was taught about vibratory centers, each echoing the primordial sounds of life in the universe. The lowest center is the navel that controls all human functions. Above it, the heart, so each might understand the difference between good and evil. Next is the throat so that each person might sing songs to honor life itself. Then, the brain where each has a duty to understand the plan of all creation. Finally, the top of the head, an open door through which we all receive life from the Creator.

Like Hindu Charkas, Carmen thought. Something she knew something about.

She marveled at how content the Hopi were without modern technologies. She hadn't sat down to watch a TV since arriving. Her cell phone remained unpacked. She remembered how close she'd been to the earth and weather and the animals at Wide Waters growing up.

"Where do these people come from?" she asked Seamus.

"Originally from China," he said. "They see the White Man as lost."

"Perhaps we are."

"They think so because we use our throats to conduct business, seek riches, accumulate things," Seamus explained. "For the Hopi, understanding your place is the meaning of life."

After a week of preparation, Carmen received instructions from Chosposi himself.

"We are all characters in the same cosmic drama," he taught her.

"What does the drama mean?" Carmen asked.

"The question is always the same," Chosposi said. "How can you play two roles: One as the cosmic spirit of all mankind. The other, your own temporal existence?"

Carmen understood. Experience the eternal in the present moment. She had lived life as an avatar in exactly that way. But as Digital Darling, retaining a clear idea of her own individuality had proved elusive. Perhaps she would succeed this time.

When the stars were properly aligned in mid-November, the villagers prepared for the secretive ceremony. Carmen fasted, was bathed, and then isolated from all others so that the spirits might visit her. She was placed in a huge underground pit, or kiva, and sat cross-legged on a raised altar wearing only body paint. The kiva symbolized the underworld from which she would emerge. Patrols were sent out to keep all others, especially a nervous Seamus, away. A small fire lighted the kiva.

At midnight, four white-robed men symbolizing the four winds climbed down a ladder into the kiva. They wore four-pointed star masks and their bodies were painted ash white. They made low humming sounds that gradually rose in pitch and volume until their voices filled the cavern. They danced around the fire for what seemed like hours as Carmen watched, growing dizzy. Then they suddenly extinguished the fire, demonstrating how quickly we are all thrown into darkness. With much yelling and screaming they rushed back up the ladder. Atop, they were received by the clan's three eldest women, who descended into the kiva and carried Carmen to the home of her godmother, who washed her hair in nine successive bowls of yucca suds. Reinvigorated, Carmen was ready for the final step in her initiation, the challenge Seamus had mentioned: She was to visit a special cave at the mouth of the Grand Canyon to obtain a gift of salt for the villagers. It was a long trek and arduous descent.

Seamus didn't want her to go, but Carmen reminded him that she would remain forever a fledgling, too spiritually weak to fly, if she did not succeed.

She was gone for two days. Seamus almost went mad waiting for her to return.

Carmen made the pilgrimage barefoot and returned

lame, but with the precious salt. Amid much joy and congratulations she was crowned Tuwaletstiwa, that is, The Sun Standing Up. It was the name by which she became Seamus' blood sister, Hopi partner, and for all intents and purposes, his wife.

Chapter 49
The Oprah effect

North finally agreed with Pipes that Digital Darling affair had left some lose ends that needed tidying up before re-election season. Pipes had been getting calls from mainstream media asking whether the blogosphere's contention that the events which had transpired at Wide Waters and the sudden death of a little old lady in Damariscotta and the mob-style slaughter of a prominent Weston banker might be somehow connected. Investigative reporters, some with huge audiences, wanted to know.

Pipes had done well with his virus movie, so North gave him the go-ahead to use the same tactic to smooth over the tragedy that had unfolded along the shores of Big Sebago Lake.

Like Bartholomew, Pipes had had the raid filmed, too—from the helicopters and from helmet-cams. In his version, the raid took on the flavor of a rescue mission. The forces of good against a heavily armed band of off-the-reservation Indians.

Pipes' version showed how the Indians had ignored

initial offers to avoid bloodshed. How Brand had fired first, and how the government's plans for a peaceful resolution were dashed when its agents had been slaughtered in the roundabout crossfire. His teleplay had close-ups of young, clean-shaven white men writhing in agony and twisted faces of brown men screaming gibberish.

The intensity of the Winnebago war room was there, too.

Poncho barking orders.

Men doing their duty.

"These soldiers are the best America has," said the narrator, none other than Eliza North. "They know what it means to be a patriot."

In Pipes' movie, sympathetic, graven-faced Mainers gave heartwarming speeches about how tragic and avoidable it all was...if only. "You can be sure," Eliza pledged with her silky reassuring voice, "those responsible for the death of this great humanitarian, a renown scholar and inventor, will be brought to justice."

The video ran intact and in snippets on dozens of TV channels, hundreds of blogs and web sites. It was backed up by press materials from the White House containing select details of Bartholomew's checkered career, and discreet talking points disguised as authoritative quotes. There was no mention of Aunt Lottie or James Holliston. None of the Passamaquoddy were interviewed.

The story went viral. It was left to a handful of Digital Darling disciples and the Passamaquoddy themselves to keep the outrage alive by relentlessly asking: How does the house of a private citizen, a retired academic at that, become the target of a deadly Blackhawk attack in the first place?

Or, more directly, just how afraid of our government were we now supposed to be?

————————

From a veranda at the Hotel Panaromos Village on the quiet north shore of Mykonos Island, Day-to-day Dave entered the dark web intending to design and transmit a version of Wide Waters story that equated the raid to Waco and Ruby Ridge. He hitched a ride on an Iranian router. He mixed bits and pieces of the raid tapes with Carmen's final show, then embellished both with news clips of Holliston's and Aunt Lottie's passing that revealed the hypocrisy of the government's argument. But his efforts went unrewarded. It was too late to recapture the nobility of the idea that was Digital Darling. To rekindle a more skin and bones, more elemental take on what comprises consciousness. These were real people who had died, Dave insisted, not just an avatar. But for most, when freedom of travel was restored, Digital Darling could go away, too. She was off the Internet for a reason, wasn't she?

Of those who did pick up the dialog, Dave was discouraged by how many sympathized with the government's vague contention that the Passamaquoddy may have been acting out of revenge toward the Brands—the family that had appropriated their lands some two centuries before.

Dave had lost his mentor and maybe even his

country. When he blogged about the parade in Boston, four out of five only wanted to talk about the naked look-alikes.

Chapter 50
Pump and dump

"**F**unny how things work out," Wilkins said to Barronson several weeks later.

They both had their feet up on the railing of the Truman Balcony looking south over the Mall. It was Thanksgiving, but still warm in the nation's capital.

"You did a good job with that mess up in Maine," Wilkins congratulated him. "Planting agents in the local bars to spread stories about what had happened. Nice touch."

"Thanks. And G-20 went away?"

"Like a rash on a baby's ass. We just showed them the first month's take on tourism. Hell, every central bank was devaluing their own currency anyway."

"You have to admire Disney," Pipes said. "They know how to move people."

Pipes opened another beer and helped himself to another slice of pizza. He had a dozen reasons to feel good. *TIME* magazine had named North "Man of the Year." The NSA had come off a winner, if mysteriously so, as had the CDC. Ms. Navaho had been appointed international hostess for the president's ambitious tourism plan, now on schedule to reinstate America as the world's number one destination. Even that odd photographer Casaba Rendor had gotten a gig on some late-night reality show.

Stay-cations were out. Eco-tourism, adventure tourism, agri-tourism, space tourism were all the rage.

Against all odds, American had landed right side up.

"What's next?" Wilkins asked. "You sticking around?"

"Like to try the other side of the street," Pipes said.

"Alex might take that the wrong way," Wilkins replied.

"Alex likes being the hero in a story everyone wants to hear. I can help him from the outside, too," Pipes said, handing Wilkins the last beer.

Chapter 51
Two years later...

A t the outset, the land around the manor house at Wide Waters had been cleared for two hundred yards in all directions. This provided from the widow's walk an unobstructed view south and west over the lake and north and east across the open fields. In the early years, the widow's walk and cleared land also offered protection against marauding Indians. Seven generations of Brands had defended and improved the homestead since its initial construction in the late 1700s. In its heyday, the great home boasted a 6000-volume library, a wine cellar that was the envy of every restaurateur down east, a museum-quality collection of mounted horns, heads and antlers, more carved wooden mantels, stained glass, white marble and ivory than an Italian palazzo, and thanks to Bartholomew, a spectacular communications complex and computer laboratory as sophisticated as anything at Bell Labs.

Much of it lay in ashes when Carmen and Seamus returned. They bulldozed the rest and Carmen planted a glorious perennial garden that flourished in the spot.

Before scattering, the Indians had buried Bartholomew in a plot near the berry fields. Carmen consecrated that with more flowers. She and Seamus made a home for themselves in the guest cottage, eventually rebuilding the barn and corrals and starting a lively business providing homes to unwanted and orphaned animals.

They also grieved.

Time passed, and so did the burdensome sadness. They reconnected with nature and increasingly with each other.

Carmen came up with a "tell," a tied satin bow at her breasts. She put one on blouses and pullovers on a bathing suit, and her pajamas. There was no pattern to when a bow might appear. Sometimes she would surprise Seamus wearing one three days in a row. Sometimes she would tease him, waiting almost a week. When it was there, she was an advertisement for pleasure and some-times he would take her the minute she came through the front door, or on top of the workbench he'd set up in the spare room, scattering the hand tools, knocking over the water buckets, both of them oblivious to the mounds of un-worked clay. Sometimes she pushed him hard up against the warm kitchen stove and made him satisfy her that way. In the summer she was always barefoot with the bow. In winter they made a game of unlacing her boots. Seamus knew everything about her toes.

One warm fall day, Carmen was in from picking veg-etables and trimming them up on the kitchen chopping block when the phone rang. A man's voice she didn't recognize said: "My name is Barronson. I was communications director in the White House during your reign as Digital Darling."

"I know who you are," Carmen snapped. "What do you want?"

"I want to offer you a job. In the media."

"My media days are over," Carmen brushed the suggestion away. She took a big hack at some beet tops.

"I now host a TV show called *PipeLine*, Barronson went on. "An insider's look at Washington, if you will. We interview important people. Sometimes I do the interviews, but more often we have a guest interviewer, the more famous the better."

"I'm not famous."

"You're still Top Ten on the web. I checked."

"And who would I interview?" Carmen asked, scrubbing some potatoes furiously.

"President Alexander North," Pipes said.

Carmen dropped the spuds and laughed. "Surely you can find someone who admires the man?"

"North has offered to announce his candidacy for a second term on my show," Barronson went on. "As a personal favor."

"Why would you, or the president, want me there?"

"Actually, Ms. Brand, both the president and I thought it was a great idea. Old adversaries meet again. Audience appeal. You understand."

"I was promised we'd be left alone."

"Don't say no yet. Think about it."

◄►◄►

They sat at the small kitchen table in the guesthouse eating breakfast.

Seamus said to her, "I had trouble with the government before we met."

"I know,' Carmen said.

"Dave?"

"Yes. But we never got the whole story."

"I'll tell you the whole story. I did well in ROTC. I had studied Russian in college. I was promised a desk job inside the NSA."

"They lied."

"Sort of. Turned out nobody cared much about the Russians anymore," Seamus continued. "I was retrained as a marksman and converted to field operations—in Nogales on our side of the border. There was a rumor that a Middle Eastern group was training Arabs to speak Spanish and smuggling them across in Arizona. We were on night parole a lot. The border leaks everywhere. The surveillance technology at the fence never worked. Agents just started shooting people. It was dark. It was easier. It became part of the mission."

"But you didn't?"

"Didn't. Couldn't. Worse, I reported it."

"You were banished to Sturbridge."

"You and Dave got the dope on that?"

"We guessed right."

"It burnt a hole in me. But Sturbridge helped heal that."

"I had a high school friend who dropped the winning touchdown pass in the big game," Carmen said. "Same thing?"

"Same thing with guns," Seamus said.

He paused and finished his tale. "They lie all the time. They kill just like the mob, or the Bulgarians, or the Arabs, whoever. You reach a point when you can't tell if your cause is more just, or just a different cause. It's all terrorism if you're the target."

"So you stayed around because Dave and I were searching for the truth?"

"No. I stayed because I fell in love with you. I didn't think the show would make any difference."

To Seamus' surprise, Carmen suddenly grew dark.

"We didn't make any difference," she said. "North got everything he wanted. He's a shoe-in for reelection."

"You haven't decided yet, have you?" Seamus asked.

Carmen didn't answer. She didn't know how much fight was left inside her. She had become Digital Darling at first to please her father. Then the thrill of the ride. If she got to live in Boston, so much the better. If the Feds got hurt and social justice was served along the way that served them right. They had extinguished a brilliant mind. Who knows what her father might have created besides an enlightened travel host. Her father had taught her that life on-camera, on-keyboard, on-line was the only thing of consequence. That what you did in the privacy of your own life didn't matter. Now, for the first time, she disagreed with her father. She was content now. Back on the land she loved. Back in Seamus' arms. That was her truth. Who cared about the world's truth? Besides, wasn't it someone else's turn?

Carmen got up from the table. "Up for a ride?" she asked.

They went to the barn, saddled up Dobson and Peppermint and rode away from the lake shore, across the burnished fields of late fall and into the pine and birch woods to Carmen's secret spot. They wrapped themselves in a blanket and lay in each other's arms for much of the day.

At one point Carmen said, "When I was a little girl my mother dressed me up for holidays. The Fourth of July Girl. The Valentine Girl. More than once, the Easter Bunny. I liked it. I liked the idea that you can become someone else. I liked being Digital Darling."

"You succeeded as Digital Darling," Seamus said. "You proved what one voice could do. Your father is proud."

—————————⇒⊗⋘—————————

The next morning Carmen was up at dawn. "No script," she said the minute Pipes picked up the phone. "No bullshit. I get to ask whatever I want. And no seven-second delays."

"I'm sure we can work it out," Pipes said.

"I'm no digital fantasy," Carmen warned. "You deal with the real me this time."

—————————⇒⊗⋘—————————

North agreed to come to Maine for the announcement. It would look good getting out of D.C., Pipes advised. "Most people consider it a sewer. The air in Maine is nice and fresh."

They met Carmen at a local CBS station in Portland.

Pipes sat stage left in a director's chair and introduced a special edition of his popular political show. He praised President North as the perfect balance between an idealistic and practical leader, a credit to his country and his generation. A man who kept a keen eye on what was morally right, and then did what worked best for the nation. He met difficult challenges with boldness and imagination. This guaranteed him, Pipes argued, a place among our best presidents. And the right to continue his work.

Pipes was no less effusive introducing Carmen. Today, he said we're joined by the beauty and the brains behind the most celebrated, most widely pixilated personage in modern media. Carmen Brand was Digital Darling, the woman who insisted that it was time for every American to ask themselves, what is my civic duty? What does it mean to be a true patriot?

Carmen and North sat center stage. She could tell that the president was in an expansive mood. Why not? What accolades were left to be bestowed? What might he do for an encore? She wanted on one hand to wipe the smugness from his smile. On the other hand, she considered the cost. She balanced her idyllic life against the niggling sense of guilt she felt about the deal she'd made with Ms. Navaho. A deal the government had so far kept, but what did that prove? As Seamus might have said, it was the rooster guaranteeing the chickens would be safe.

Carmen wrestled with her decision. She had more to lose now than she'd had when leaving Maine. The potential consequences felt more permanent. Then a disturbing thought crossed her mind. Suppose this was the moment her father had envisioned? For her to upstage North, not as some dazzling visage, but as herself, the real Carmen Brand. Suppose they agreed, after all, about what was important? But how could he have anticipated this moment? She took a deep breath as camera two lit up green in front of her. Round Two of the President vs. the People began.

She turned to North and thanked the president for coming.

"You know who my father was, right?" she asked.

"Brilliant man," President North replied. "With a wise daughter, no doubt." He smiled warmly at Carmen but she heard the warning in his words.

"Thank you, Mr. President," Carmen said, flashing her own telegenic smile. She wet her lips, leaned in closer and asked her next question.

"I bid you to the one-man revolution—the only revolution that's coming."

– Robert Frost

www.ingramcontent.com/pod-product-compliance
Lightning Source LLC
Chambersburg PA
CBHW070444260626
47161CB00004B/1192